Charlie and Me

Charlie and Me

MARK LOWERY

Piccadilly
PRESS

First published in Great Britain in 2018 by
PICCADILLY PRESS
80–81 Wimpole St, London W1G 9RE
www.piccadillypress.co.uk

A CIP catalogue record for this book is available
from the British Library.

ISBN: 978-1-84812-622-0
also available as an ebook

1

Printed and bound by Clays Ltd, St Ives Plc

Piccadilly Press is an imprint of Bonnier Zaffre Ltd,
a Bonnier Publishing company
www.bonnierpublishing.com

For my family

LEAPING DOLPHIN

Your life is a leaping dolphin
Bursting out from
Blackness,
Blankness
Into brilliant sunshine.
Twisting,
Flipping,
Straining
In whatever direction
You choose.
And scattering
Infinity and one
Tiny droplets of water,
Each one briefly containing
A tiny, distorted reflection
Of yourself.
You are a leaping dolphin.
A glorious example
Of what it means
To be alive.

By Martin Tompkins
Aged 13

STAGE 1

886 PLUNGINGTON ROAD TO PRESTON STATION

VIA FAROOK'S SUPERNEWS

1.5 MILES

WALKING

BISCUITS AND BELLY BUTTONS

My little brother Charlie's sitting cross-legged on the floor of the corner shop, humming with his eyes closed. He does this kind of thing a lot.

'Hurry up,' I say, giving him a friendly shove with my raggedy old Reebok. 'We've got a train to catch.'

Charlie wipes his nose on his sleeve. 'Gizza minute, Marty,' he replies. 'I'm just charging up the laser in my belly button.'

He *says* this kind of thing a lot too.

My brother Charlie doesn't have a laser in his belly button. I know this for a fact. Not that I've ever *studied* it. But if you share a small bedroom with your brother for ten years then you end up pretty well acquainted with his whole body whether you like it or not.

Charlie isn't like ordinary kids. He's one in a million. In fact, he's one in a *Charlillion*. A Charlillion, by the way, is a number he invented, which is one more than infinity. I tried to explain to him that you can't have one more than infinity. Infinity means it goes on forever. Charlie called me a banana-brain. He can be very childish when he wants to be.

At poetry club in school, Mr Hendrix sometimes plays a game to warm up. You've got to talk about a topic for thirty seconds without stopping or repeating yourself. Here's what I'd say about Charlie:

'Lazy eye, massive head, snores like a hippo, often ill, weird taste in food, terrible memory, always out of breath cos of his asthma, weedy, cheeky, can't do anything for himself or concentrate for more than two seconds, brain's inside out, no understanding of danger. My absolute best mate in the whole entire world.'

I'd have to stop there. You could talk about Charlie for a Charlillion seconds if you wanted to, and you'd never run out of things to say.

'Which biscuits do you fancy?' I ask him. Mr Farook is watching us carefully from behind the counter. Each time I glance over he's there, leaning right back so he can see along the aisle. I smile at him but his face stays blank. I'm starting to feel queasy.

Charlie pushes his milk-bottle specs up on his nose and squints at me through his lazy eye. His good eye has a Peppa Pig patch on it so that his lazy one learns to work harder. *Peppa Pig* is one of Charlie's favourite shows, despite him being at least six years older than the average viewer. 'Why can't we have one of the biscuits from your rucksack?'

I clutch the rucksack to my chest, squeezing the hard corners of the omni-special-leftover-from-Christmas biscuit tin that I pinched from home. Of course Charlie saw me nick the biscuits. He sees everything, even though his eyes are rubbish. Maybe he's not got a laser in his belly button. Maybe it's a CCTV camera.

'They're special,' I say. 'They're for when we get there.'

'Get where?'

'Where we're going.'

I don't want to tell him where we're going till we're on the train. He'll only get excited. And trust me, an excited Charlie is not what I need in my life at quarter to seven on a Saturday morning. Imagine filling a puppy with blue Smarties and Lemon Fanta, then bouncing it on a trampoline: that's Charlie when he's excited.

'Are there any of those chocolate wheels in the tin?' he asks.

'Course,' I say.

'What about the hefty thick ones in the golden foil? They're my favourites. Ninety per cent chocolate. Five per cent biscuit.'

'What's the other five per cent?' I ask, just because he's always got a weird answer.

Charlie sniffs hard. 'Dreams.'

Told you. Brain inside out.

He settles on a packet of Jammy Dodgers from the shelf (an excellent choice) and we go to pay.

When I get my wallet out I accidentally flash my wad of twenty-pound notes, which is a mistake. Mr Farook's big furry eyebrows shoot up his forehead. The guy's like a bloodhound for money. The police should use him to sniff out where gangsters hide their cash.

'Going somewhere special?' he says, nodding at my rucksack.

I'm trying to figure out how to answer this when Charlie butts in.

'Switzerland,' he says seriously. 'I'm getting my belly-button laser upgraded.'

By the time Mr Farook can reply, we're out on the street.

'Nice work, boss,' I say, giving Charlie a fist-bump. He gives me his cheekiest, squintiest, one-eyed grin and we set off walking to the train station.

WALRUS FLOPPING

One thing everyone needs to know about Charlie: he is a miracle.

He was born well early – about fifteen weeks before he was meant to be. Mum and Dad never let me visit him when he was in hospital because I was only three, but I've seen a photo: a minuscule, scrawny red alien in a fish tank, with a woolly hat on and eyelids like ping-pong balls. There's a tube sprouting out of his nose and wires attached to his chest and machines blinking all around him. Dad's finger is in the corner of the shot and it's almost as long as Charlie's whole body.

They kept him in hospital for three months because he was so sick. A machine had to breathe for him because his lungs were a pair of useless wet sponges. His heart kept breaking down so he had to have four emergency operations on it. And, after all that, he caught a really serious infection from one of his breathing tubes. A couple of times the doctors told Mum and Dad to go in and say goodbye because *this could be The Night*.

It makes me feel sick when I think how close he came to . . . you know . . .

But, somehow, he fought and fought and stayed alive. The doctors thought it was so incredible that they even got the newspapers to come and write about him. We've still got the clippings in a frame on the mantelpiece: 'Meet Charlie the Miracle Baby'; 'Fighting Fit Charlie Back from the Dead'; 'Alive and Kicking'.

The day he finally came home is one of my earliest memories. I can picture Dad holding me on one knee with Charlie in the crook of his other arm. 'Meet your baby brother, big guy,' he said, dark rings round his eyes and his voice catching in his throat. 'You're gonna have to look after him.'

So I guess I always have: holding his hand to cross the road; cutting up his food and tying his laces for him because he's so clumsy; making sure his bag's packed in the morning because he always forgets what he needs; biting the bruises out of his apples because he's got a weird thing about them; teaching him to throw and catch even though he's rubbish at it; sitting with him through all of his millions of appointments and check-ups at the hospital.

A few years ago, Mum told me I was the best big brother in the world. It was cool of her to say so, but I don't see it like that. Charlie's a right laugh, but he can be like a lost kitten sometimes – bumbling through life all confused and unaware of what's going on around him. It's not like I'm a good person or anything. I just *have* to help him out.

Still, Charlie doesn't always want me to help him. He likes to do things his own way. Mum says he's a free spirit, but I'd call him a loony. In the nicest possible way of course.

Even when he was a baby he was like that. It took him ages to learn to walk, but he never let it hold him back. He used to do this strange lop-sided crawl – the walrus flop, Dad called it – which was surprisingly fast. One time when he was nearly two, Mum put him in his travel cot (aka 'The Cage', because it was the only way to keep him still) and nipped upstairs to do something.

When she came back down ten minutes later, he'd disappeared. The front door was open. She thought he'd been snatched and she ran outside in a blind panic. And there he was – walrus-flopping across the road, cars slamming on their brakes and swerving out of the way.

Trying to piece together what'd happened afterwards, Mum reckoned he'd been bored so he'd bitten his way through the seam of the plastic mesh wall of the travel cot. Then he'd yanked the sides apart to make an escape hole, walrus-flopped across the lounge, somehow opened the front door and made a break for it.

Then there was the day when he was four and he decided he didn't like his eyebrows. He said they were freaking him out. So, being Charlie, he shaved them clean off with Dad's razor. There was blood everywhere. He looked like he'd been attacked with a potato peeler.

And how about when he played the innkeeper in the

school nativity play? We still watch the film of it every Christmas. He only had one line to remember – 'Sorry. No room at the inn.' – but this is Charlie we're talking about. After telling Mary and Joseph that they could stay in the honeymoon suite (who knows where he got that from?) and that the donkey could have its own room, he pulled the baby Jesus out from under Mary's dress, held Him up by His ankle and announced: 'Behold! The King of the shoes!' On the film you can almost hear the teacher slapping her forehead off-screen as she says, 'It's King of the Jews. And put Him back – you're a day early.'

INVISIBLE BOYS

After leaving Farook's, we walk quickly along Plungington Road towards the station. It's still insanely early so the late-September air is cool and there aren't many people about – a few shopkeepers and cafe owners pulling up their shutters and setting up their signs; a couple of students staggering home from the night before.

I try not to look at any of them. I'm expecting someone to stop us and ask us what we're doing out at this time, or if our parents know where we are, or to call the police. But no one seems to notice us. They've all got their own lives to think about. We're invisible.

This is a good thing. We need to get to the train station and onto a train without Mum and Dad realising we're gone. If they find out what I'm doing, they'll go proper mental. They're so protective of Charlie it's unbelievable. He's not even allowed out on his scooter without an armed guard and a full set of injections.

As we walk, I start to relax a bit. Every step takes us closer to safety. Once we've got our tickets we'll be on our way.

Break things down into little bits and they don't seem so scary any more.

'Jammy Dodger?' says Charlie, offering me the packet.

I take one and we chink them in mid-air like glasses of wine. 'Breakfast of champions,' I say.

For a short while we walk alongside each other, crunching our biscuits and not saying anything. It's rare to have silence when Charlie's around and it doesn't last long.

'You still haven't told me where we're going,' he says. He's found a stick and he's dragging it along some railings outside a church.

'Somewhere good, I promise,' I say, but it's still too soon to let him know. I need to change the subject. 'Shall I test you on your times tables?'

I always try to help him with his homework. He struggles at school because he can't focus on things and he's a bit hyperactive. Mum says this is common with kids who were born early. She's always having rows with the teachers about it, because he can't be expected to learn like everyone else, can he? And if they let him use his imagination instead of trying to stuff his poor little head full of useless information, then maybe he'd have a chance in life.

She's very sensitive when it comes to Charlie. And she's sort of right – people think he's thick, but in some ways he's mega-smart. His brain's just wired up differently, that's all.

Even so, the teachers *have* got a point. When he was in

Year Three, he brought a letter home saying: 'Charlie did not complete today's spelling test because he was pretending to be a tortoise.' Dad thought this was hilarious and stuck it on the fridge.

'Times tables? On a Saturday?' says Charlie, flinging the stick down. The baggy sleeves of his jumper swing round afterwards. 'Child cruelty! I'm calling the RSPCA.'

'What?' I say. 'The *animal* charity?'

'Yeah,' replies Charlie, as though this is what he meant all along. 'I'll tell 'em you keep a . . . a pig in a shoe box and . . . you throw darts at it and you make it smoke cigarettes. They'll lock you up and then I'll be safe.'

I snigger. 'Come on. Which times table are you doing at the moment?'

'The one times table,' he says immediately. 'One one is one. Two ones are t—'

'Rubbish!' I interrupt, giving him a friendly jab in the arm. 'Nobody learns the ones. Let's do the eights. One eight is eight. Two eights are . . . ?'

Charlie looks off into the distance and scratches his head. 'Er . . . fourteen . . . ?'

'Try again.'

'Twelve . . . no, seventeen.'

'It can't be seventeen,' I sigh. I try to be patient with him, but I'm pretty good at maths and working with Charlie can get *seriously* frustrating. 'We've been through this. Seventeen's not in any tables. It's a prime number.'

This was a mistake. Straight away he's talking about something else.

'Prime number? Is that like the Prime Minister?' he says, and before I can answer he's off: 'If I was Prime Minister, I'd make everyone wear top hats.'

We reach a red light and I push the button. 'What? Why?' I say, my brain struggling to catch up.

'I like 'em. Plus then I'd be taller than everyone.'

'But they'd all be wearing top hats too.'

He thinks for a second. 'Yeah. But only the Prime Minister would be allowed to wear high heels.'

'In-*credible*,' I say, puffing out my cheeks and pressing the button again. Without warning, Charlie steps out into the road even though the man's only just turned red. I drag him back moments before a car roars past. Luckily I'm always expecting him to do things like this. 'Careful!'

No understanding of danger whatsoever.

'Hey, Marty,' he says, switching the conversation again like nothing just happened, 'why did we have to leave without telling Mum and Dad?'

I bite my lip. I knew he'd ask this sooner or later so I've already prepared my answer. 'I didn't want to wake them. Dad didn't get in from work till gone midnight.'

He screws up his face. 'Are you sure we're allowed out this early?'

'Yep. 'S fine. Anyway, I'll text them when we're on the train.'

'How will you do that?' he sniffs.

'Phone of course.'

'But I saw you hide your phone in your sock drawer when I was getting dressed.'

I say nothing, focusing hard on my finger as it jabs the button again and again. I told you. He sees *everything*. CCTV in his belly button. And probably satellite dishes on his nipples.

'Why *would* you do that, Marty?' he continues. 'It's like you don't want anyone to be able to get hold of us. And if you *are* going to hide something, you really should *close* the drawer afterwards, you know.'

The green man appears and I pull Charlie across the road. 'Have another Jammy Dodger,' I mutter. I need to keep calm and positive so, for the rest of the journey into town, I try to think up a poem in my head.

YOU ONLY LIVE ONCE

A Haiku

You only live once
So you might as well just eat
Biscuits for breakfast.

By Martin Tompkins
Aged 13

STAGE 2

PRESTON RAILWAY STATION TICKET OFFICE TO THE
TOILETS ON PLATFORM THREE AND BACK AGAIN

TWO HUNDRED AND FIFTY METRES (APPROX.)

WALKING

THE STATION

I'm not happy about how busy the station is: three young soldiers pretending not to struggle with their massive duffle bags; a homeless guy sitting on the floor between the ticket windows, head down between his knees and cap by his feet; two confused foreign students squinting at the departure screen; a cluster of Preston North End fans off to an away game – some of them glugging cans of cider, even though it's only just seven o'clock in the morning. And, worst of all, two police officers watching them carefully from twenty metres away.

In the queue for tickets I take my notebook out of my bag, but I can't find the piece of paper I tucked in there with all the train times on it. I check again, then double-check inside the rucksack. For a moment I think I've seen it. There's a loose bit of paper, but when I pull it out I'm disappointed; it's just this mileage chart thing I printed off that tells you how much distance there is between all the towns in the UK. Whenever we're going on a long journey, I like to know how far we've travelled and how far's left to go. Like I said, everything seems easier when you break it down into little bits. Even so, it's not going to help me know which train to catch.

Great start.

I put my notebook and the mileage chart away again and notice my hands are trembling. All the people – especially the police – are making me nervous.

Keep calm. Look normal.

I reach the window and smile at the woman behind the counter. Her badge says '*Sue – Trainee*'. Big brown hair. Pink lipstick. Round face. Charlie's off to the side; he's found a timetable-holder that spins and he's whizzing it round like a roundabout.

What am I meant to do now? Sue leans forward and nods as if to say, *Get on with it.* I take a deep breath and speak into the microphone. 'Hi, Sue,' I say. *Am I meant to use her name?* 'We'd . . . er . . . like to go to St Bernards.'

The microphone amplifies my voice, like it's announcing where we're going to the police behind me. The last thing I need is *them* sniffing around asking me questions.

Sue's painted-on eyebrows rise up her forehead. 'As in St Bernards in *Cornwall?*'

She says *Cornwall* like it's somewhere near Jupiter.

I'm about to say yes when Charlie looks over. 'ST BERNARDS?!' he cries. 'No way! Oh wow!'

Before I can stop him, his jumper's up over his face and he's running round the forecourt like he's just scored at Wembley.

I told you he'd get excited.

'Don't worry about my brother. He's got an inside-out brain,' I say to Sue, rubbing my neck and trying not to look agitated.

She looks at me like *I'm* the weird one. 'You *do* know how far that is . . . ?'

I peep over my shoulder. Charlie is looping around the foreign students, arms out like an aeroplane. They're too busy to have noticed him yet, which *would* be funny except for the fact that sooner or later someone *will* notice him. I was hoping we could keep this low-key.

'Three hundred and seventy miles,' I reply, turning back to Sue and doing my best to remain calm and level. 'I checked on my mileage chart. We went there on holiday last year with our mum and dad. Charlie chose it because he liked the name: he said it sounds like one of those dogs. You know – the massive ones they use in the mountains to rescue people. But it turns out it's a lovely place. They've got a lighthouse. Have you ever been?'

I'm talking too much. *Shut up. Shut up.*

Sue taps away at her computer. 'No, sadly not . . . Single or return?' she says. There's a hint of bored frustration in her voice.

'Oh,' I say. My palms are sweaty. I practised this conversation over and over in front of the mirror so I'd sound natural, but this isn't a question I'd been expecting. I push my knuckle into my eye to try to ease the throbbing pain that's building up. This isn't going to plan. 'I'm . . . er . . . not sure.'

As soon as the words come out of my mouth I realise exactly what she meant; simple question: *Are you coming back or not?* I feel like a total dunce. Sue nods towards the people behind me. 'Well, I've got a queue so . . .'

Even though I know the answer to the question now, I shuffle to the side, head down like a slapped dog. An older woman steps up to the window and starts jabbering away about quiet coaches and super-saver advances and aisle seats. There's a whole language for buying train tickets I've never heard of. How do people know all this stuff? Why don't they teach us it at school? All we learn is triangles and books and swimming and . . . *Why am I thinking about swimming?*

My whole body feels shaky, like I'm standing on top of a rickety fence in the wind. I'm taking deep breaths and trying to *normalise* myself and it's made worse because Charlie's back at my shoulder going on and on and on about how St Bernards is the best place in the world, and how he can't believe we're going back there, and will we go to the beach, and will I buy him fish and chips, and do you think we'll see the dolphin. And I can feel one of my headaches coming on because we're not even out of the station and it's all starting to go wrong, and my hands are over my ears and my eyes are clamped shut and the lights are flashing in my head.

I feel a hand on my shoulder, which makes me jump, and when I turn round a policewoman's standing there asking me if I'm all right. I swallow down the huge egg in my throat and splutter, 'Yes, thanks. Just a headache. Need to splash some water on my face.'

And I manage to hold it together long enough to grab Charlie and stumble down the ramp to the toilets on platform three.

ST BERNARDS

Of course I knew Charlie would get excited. It's not his fault. I mean, he's the whole reason for us going to St Bernards in the first place.

As I said, we went there on holiday last summer and it was amazing. This was fourteen months ago: when we still did things as a family. Back before things got a bit crummy at home. Back before Dad started working a Charlillion hours a week and Mum started sleeping in.

It was a Friday night and we'd just broken up from school. Mum was preparing for the holiday by hoovering the whole house. Dad joked she was making it clean for the burglars. I'd just finished helping Charlie pack his bag (*No, I had to tell him, you can't put an open carton of yogurt in there. I don't care if Big Ted gets hungry . . .*) when Dad called us together on the sofa. He said that now we were getting older we might not have many more family holidays so we should make it a good one – a proper adventure. After all, it'd taken him two years to save up for this one, so being miserable was not an option.

Charlie saluted with his tongue sticking out. 'Yes, sir!' he barked.

Dad sniggered and ruffled Charlie's hair.

We set off at half ten that night to miss the traffic – all four of us crammed into our little Fiesta with the roof rack on and 'We're All Going on a Summer Holiday' blaring out of the stereo. The back end of the car was so weighed down it was practically dragging along the tarmac. Charlie was bouncing about on his booster seat like a flea with an itchy backside. Munching sweets. Singing. Telling jokes. Me, I guess I prefer to sit back a bit and let him shine. I had a road atlas on my knees and I slowly followed the M6 south with my finger, checking off the junctions as we passed them and flicking back to the mileage chart at the front to see how far to go till the next big town.

About 2 a.m. we pulled up at the services to sleep in the car. It was just like Dad said – a proper adventure. Well, for a couple of hours anyway. Till some security guard knocked on the car window and told us to cough up twenty quid or bog off.

We bogged off, with Charlie mooning out of the rear window. Dad said he was awake now so he might as well push on through. He's used to night shifts driving the forklift, so it was no big deal to him. The rest of us dozed in fits and starts, and we arrived red-eyed in St Bernards at half seven in the morning. Our caravan wasn't going to be ready till the afternoon, so Dad parked up and we had a stretch, then wandered off to find some breakfast.

The town was just waking up – the smell of fresh bread from bakeries. Shopkeepers dragging racks of flip-flops and beach balls out of shops called Wild Bill's Surf Shack or Bob's Budget Beach Hut. Street cleaners emptying bins and aiming half-hearted kicks at the cocky seagulls that scrounged around the cobblestones.

We'd been roaming about for a few minutes before we caught a glimpse of the ocean – a narrow strip of blue between two cottages. 'Might as well have a peek,' Dad said. We followed a steep lane until it opened out onto the seafront, and WOW!

It was incredible.

The town nestled above a bay about a quarter of a mile wide. It was a perfect semicircle, like the sea had taken a great big bite out of the land. Colourful cottages seemed to tumble higgledy-piggledy down the slope towards it. The tide was right in and fishing boats bobbed up and down on a sparkling sheet of turquoise. To our right, the bay was fringed by jagged rocks that concealed the rest of the coast. At the far side over to the left, an old stone jetty stretched out to sea, with a small white lighthouse perched at the end of it.

Dad whistled.

Mum squeezed his hand and said, 'Beautiful.'

'What are they looking at?' said Charlie, squinting at a huddle of people on the other side of the road. There were about seven of them standing by the railings and pointing out to sea.

Charlie didn't wait for an answer. He darted across the road, right in front of a car that screeched to a halt just in time. The rest of us chased after him. On the far pavement, Mum grabbed him by the arm. 'Don't you ever do that again. I couldn't bear—'

But Charlie wasn't listening. 'Wow!' he said, pointing past Mum. 'Look at that!'

'What?' said Mum, her fingers instinctively relaxing as she turned to look.

Charlie wriggled out of her grasp, peeled off his eye patch and pressed himself up against the railings. 'That! Behind that big blue boat. Next to the dinghy.'

POETRY

I've been sitting on the lid of the toilet for five minutes, just breathing in and out with my head pressed against the cold metal wall. This eventually calms me down, in spite of the horrible smell in here.

Things got a bit wobbly at the ticket office, but I managed to avoid a total disaster and everything's OK now.

Except it's not.

Not really. I've sneaked out of my house, kidnapped my brother and now we're running away to the far end of the country for the weekend. If – sorry, *when* – Mum and Dad find out, they'll murder me. That's if the police on the station don't arrest me first.

I rub my face and sit up straight. *Pull yourself together.* We've made it here, so we've successfully accomplished stage one. The hardest part is the next bit – buying the tickets and getting on the train. Once we do that we're on our way.

I pull the notebook with the picture of a dolphin on the front out of my rucksack. The book's almost full – maybe eight more pages left – so it takes a while to flick through to a blank page. I fold back the cover and jot down the poem I'd been thinking of on the way into town. A haiku. Five syllables. Seven syllables. Five syllables. Just like Mr Hendrix taught in poetry club. There's something neat about the symmetry of it that reassures me that everything's all right. The poem itself is a stupid one about biscuits. Not one of my best. But writing it down and concentrating on the tip of my biro as it moves across the page makes my worries melt away.

There's a knock on the cubicle door. Charlie. 'Have you fallen in?'

I slip the book back into the rucksack and open the door. I could hear him messing about with the hand dryers the whole time I've been in here so I wasn't worried about him. He loves a good toilet.

'Word up, brother,' I say, feeling a lot chirpier now.

We stride back up the ramp to the ticket window. Making up poems always sorts me out, even though it's not like I'm brilliant at it. Mr Hendrix reckons it's the best way to get stuff out of your brain. He says that when he's stressed he writes poems standing on his head. I don't reckon he'd fancy doing that in a filthy railway-station toilet.

'Decided yet?' says Sue. She's trying to look indulgent, like she cares, but I can tell she's bored stiff. The homeless guy by the window gives me a thumbs up and a toothless smile, like he wants me to succeed. Maybe he knows we're running away and he understands. This gives me a little confidence boost and I nod back at him.

'Two child tickets to St Bernards, coming back tomorrow,' I say to Sue in my most impressive voice. On the way back up the ramp, I noticed that the police had followed the football fans down to a platform. The forecourt feels a lot more comfortable without them around.

'This is so awesome!' says Charlie, leaning back against the wall next to the window, his arms spread out like a star.

'Two *children*?' Sue squawks. 'You mean you're travelling all that way without an adult?'

'I'm fifteen,' I lie. 'Mum said it was OK for us to go as long as we're back tomorrow.'

Sue frowns. 'I'm not sure about this. It's a really long way. I've only worked here a week. Maybe I need to speak to my manager.'

'No!' I exclaim, surprised by how my loud my voice is.

Sue moves her head back from the speaker. The homeless guy and the customer at the next window glance over at me.

'Actually I forgot. I'm an adult. One *adult* return to St Bernards,' I say, firmly but more quietly. I'm breathing so hard my breath crackles on the microphone. In. Out. *Normalise.*

Sue and Charlie both speak at the same time.

'I thought you were a child?'

'*One* adult? You can't leave me here.'

'Shut up!' I hiss.

'Pardon?' says Sue sharply.

I realise that Charlie's hidden from her view because of where he's standing.

'I was talking to my brother,' I explain, trying to smile.

'Hmm . . .' says Sue.

I press my forehead against the glass. Got to keep things under wraps this time. *Think think.* 'I'm sixteen. I just had a birthday.'

'What? Just this minute?'

'Yep. I was born at eight minutes past seven, so technically I just turned sixteen. Whoops. Silly me. Wish I'd got here ten minutes ago. Ha ha.'

I'm rambling again.

Sue frowns at me. 'What about your brother?'

'Yeah, what about me?' pipes up Charlie.

'He can stay here.'

Sue shrugs as she taps her keyboard.

'That's not fair!' cries Charlie, so I shush him.

'That'll be a hundred and seventy-seven pounds and thirty pence,' says Sue. Is it me or is her smile a bit cruel?

I feel my knees wobble. 'Really?' I squeak, gulping back the urge to cry. That'll leave me with less than ten quid. Why didn't I check the price online? I feel like such an *amateur.*

'Yes. Really,' says Sue, getting fed up now. 'If you want to travel, you've got to pay.'

I count out a stack of twenties and some coins, and drop them into the drawer. Sue pulls the lever towards her then makes a massive deal out of checking every single penny before she shoves my tickets and seventy pence change back at me. It's like a really horrible magic trick – *Marvel as I*

turn your life savings into a couple of orange-and-green bits of
card and a few pathetic coins.

'You'd better get a wiggle on,' says Sue. 'You'll be wanting the Birmingham train. Leaves platform four in two minutes.'

MOVING

You think that resting
Is peaceful.
But
When you stay still
Thoughts swarm
Round your head
Like a plague of wasps
Trapped in a jam jar,
Each one stinging
Your brain in a desperate
Attempt to be noticed.
But
When you move
You rock them to sleep,
Cute and harmless
Like a million tiny babies.

By Martin Tompkins
Aged 13

STAGE 3A

PRESTON STATION TO WOLVERHAMPTON STATION

97 MILES

TRAIN

NEAR MISS

I turn and jog away from the window. I'm trying to put the tickets into my wallet as I go, but Charlie's refusing to budge. 'Why didn't you get *me* a ticket, Marty? Why have I got to stay behind?'

'You don't!' I say, going back and putting my arm round his shoulder. 'It's better this way. The woman on the counter was going to blow our cover. And anyway, I couldn't have afforded it.'

He's still dragging his feet. 'But I can't get on a train without a ticket.'

'You'll *have* to,' I hiss. 'When the conductor comes, just hide, OK?'

Charlie's ace at hiding, as long as he doesn't have to stay still for too long. One time we played hide and seek and I couldn't find him for ages. It turned out he was trapped in the cupboard under the bathroom sink. I only realised when I heard him having an asthma attack. Dad had to free him with a hacksaw and a screwdriver.

'Now come on!' I say, and finally he starts moving. We leg

it down the ramp to the platform, but when we get there the train's not actually arrived yet. The North End fans are waiting nearby, already singing, with the police still watching on.

Charlie has a blast of his inhaler. Now I know I don't have the paper with the train times on it, I can't help but think I've forgotten other stuff as well. At least I made sure Charlie had his inhaler before he left the house; he's always getting wheezy and he needs it with him constantly. Even so, if Mum was here I'd still get a right earful for making him breathless.

I stay out of sight of the police behind a large timetable, but Charlie dodges away from me to the edge of the platform. He's leaning right out, peering into the distance. 'It's coming! It's coming!'

I stomp over and pull him away from the edge. 'Don't do that!' I say sternly. 'Stay this side of the yellow line.'

'Soz, Mum,' Charlie tuts as we move back a couple of steps.

I notice that his shoelaces are untied so I bend down to sort them out. I always tell him to choose Velcro shoes but he prefers laces, even though he's forever tripping over them and I'm usually the one who has to tie them for him.

While I'm down there, there's a gust of air and a squeak of wheels from behind me as the train snakes into the station. Charlie bursts forward towards the moving carriages. 'Gotta get on first!'

Before I can do anything, he's stumbled over me and we're both falling in slow motion, landing flat on the ground in a tangled heap inches from the edge of the platform. My heart's hammering. From down here I can see the huge wheels grinding slowly along the tracks like giant pizza slicers.

I haul myself up, then help him roughly to his feet. 'Are you trying to kill us?'

Charlie picks up his glasses, which had skittered off across the platform, and angrily puts them back on like *I've* done something wrong. 'I was trying to make sure we got a seat.'

I shake my head. The kid is utterly nuts. What kind of person tries to get onto a moving train? Even though I'm used to his crazy behaviour, my stomach is somewhere near my throat at the thought of what could've just happened. The policewoman who asked if I was OK before is looking over at us, concerned.

'Let's just get on,' I huff, pulling Charlie towards the nearest open door.

WE LOVE YOU, NORTH END

'We're off!' says Charlie as the train pulls out of the station. 'This is well exciting. I feel like a monkey with a drum kit.'

It's taken less than five minutes for him to forget that he almost got us crushed. We're edging along the aisle of the swaying carriage, struggling to stay upright as we try to find somewhere to sit. At the far end of the carriage we reach a couple of unreserved seats and plonk ourselves down. Charlie's by the window and I'm next to him, the rucksack with the biscuits in it safely on my lap.

The seats face backwards and I smile as I watch the city disappear. Within a minute or two, we're over the river then charging through open countryside. The train is sleek and fast, and it tilts into the bends like nothing could slow it down. Next to me, Charlie's got his face pressed against the glass.

Despite the near miss on the platform (or maybe *because* of it), I'm extremely happy and relieved to be on the move too. In fact, Mr Hendrix would probably say I was feeling *euphoric* right now.

Thinking of Mr Hendrix makes me remember a poem I wrote in poetry club the other day, which was all about how moving can be good for you. He said it was my best one yet; in fact he said I'd *turned a corner* with my poetry. He asked me loads of questions, then rang Mum to tell her all about it. I like Mr Hendrix, but I wasn't exactly happy about this: Mum doesn't know I even go to poetry club; it's my secret. That evening she tried to quiz me about the poem like mums do, but I could tell her heart wasn't really in it. I just grunted a few times and eventually she left me alone and went back to bed. It was four in the afternoon.

I ruffle Charlie's hair. He just practically killed us both, but I've already forgiven him. You can't stay mad at Charlie for long.

From somewhere behind us, the Preston fans start singing loudly.

> *We love you, North End!*
> *We do.*
> *We love you, North End.*
> *We do.*
> *We love you, North End.*
> *We do.*
> *Oh, North End, we love you!*

They're not being aggressive – just a bit noisy. Even so, most people in the carriage shrink into their seats or put in their earphones or pretend to be deaf. Charlie stares at them over the back of the next seat, grinning. I pull him down again before he gets us in trouble.

The fans start the chant again. And again. And again. Charlie turns to me. 'D'you think they know any other songs?'

'Just ignore it,' I say. I quite like football, but Charlie doesn't get it. Dad took us to watch Everton once and Charlie spent the whole game under his seat playing Top Trumps against himself.

After the sixteenth verse of the same song, it's wearing a bit thin. One of the fans is stumbling down the carriage, red-faced and still singing. As he goes past us, Charlie calls out to him. 'Excuse me.'

My blood freezes. Charlie still hasn't grasped that we're meant to be travelling under the radar.

The fan immediately stops singing and stares down at Charlie and then at me. He's middle-aged with a big gut squeezed into a 1980s Away shirt. Red face. Bald head. Glassy eyes. Bit rough-looking. He burps one of those deep, roaring belches that drunk people do to let everyone know they're there.

The train jerks, making him stumble forward, so he's leaning right over us and holding the seats for support. 'What?' he growls. I can smell the booze on his breath. With his belly blocking my escape, I'm feeling properly claustrophobic.

Charlie's smile doesn't fade, even though it's obvious that

he's seriously misjudged this situation. 'We were just wondering *which* team you love. We couldn't work it out.'

This is awful.

Down the carriage, the fans have stopped singing.

The big bloke grabs me – *me*, not Charlie, I'll just say here – by the collar. 'Think you're funny, you cheeky –'

'Everything all right?' says a woman's voice from behind the fan's huge bulk.

He immediately straightens up and pats my shoulder a little bit harder than necessary. 'Fine, constable,' he says. His voice is slightly slurred. 'Just chatting about the match.'

The police officer looks at me, her head tilted. I recognise her – she's the one from the station. There's a long silence and I realise she's waiting for me to agree or disagree with him.

'Like he says . . .' I whisper, the words barely coming out.

'Behave yourself or I'll put you off at the next stop,' she warns him.

The fan mumbles something at her and waddles towards the toilets. When he's safely locked inside, I pull Charlie out of his seat. Still shaking, I lead him out of the carriage, past the closed toilet door and as far away from the North End supporters as possible. I can feel the policewoman's eyes on my back as I go.

'He wasn't very friendly, was he?' whispers Charlie into my ear.

HAM AND JAM

We walk for ages to find a seat. There's a whole empty table in the quiet coach. I'm about to sit down, but quiet places and Charlie don't really mix. He lifts his leg and lets rip with the biggest fart you've ever heard. I know you're not meant to be impressed by these things, but it *is* a truly exceptional delivery and, what with everyone else being silent, it rings out like a church bell.

'Cor! Who shot a duck?' booms Charlie and a few people look at us and tut. I have to bundle him down the aisle, stifling my laughter and apologising as we go.

We finally spot two spare seats in the next coach, right by the luggage rack, and sit down. It's the last carriage before first class and this time I get the window seat. Someone has left a newspaper and an empty paper coffee cup on the little fold-out table.

Charlie plays bongos on the lid of the cup and twitches excitedly. 'You know what? This is so awesome.'

I put my jacket into the rucksack and fasten it up again. 'Just what we need,' I say with a smile.

It doesn't matter how crackers Charlie is – or how many times he nearly gets us run over or beaten up – I just enjoy doing things for him. When he's happy, I'm happy.

The train races through a station. There's a brief blur of people on benches and graffiti-covered walls then a smattering of houses before we're hurtling past green fields and bored cows again.

'I'm hungry,' he says eventually. 'Can I have one of those Christmas biscuits now?'

'I told you,' I reply, 'they're for when we get there.'

Charlie pretends to huff. 'When's that?'

'Teatime, maybe,' I say. 'What happened to the Jammy Dodgers?'

It's the kind of thing Mum would say, which immediately makes me think of her and Dad. My watch says seven thirty-five. They'll still be asleep. Dad didn't get in from work till late so he'll not wake up till eleven-ish at the earliest. Then he'll be straight back down the warehouse for the afternoon shift even though it's a Saturday. Maybe he'll stay on through the night if they ask him, which'll take him past ninety hours for the week again. And what time will Mum get up? Pick a time, any time, ladies and gentlemen. Twelve? Two? Tomorrow? Monday?

But then I have a terrible thought. Did I turn the alarm on my phone off? Oh no! If that goes off, it'll wake them up. They'll come into the bedroom. And then what? Suddenly I'm gripped with worry. They'll see the train times of course.

And the empty beds. And, downstairs, the space on the shelf where the omni-special biscuit tin should be. And my rucksack missing from the hook. And the cereal boxes left open. And that jar I left empty and unscrewed. And . . .

Gotta relax. Gotta relax, I tell myself, the words following the rhythm of the train. We're on the move. We got through the tricky bit. It's not like they can come and get us, is it? I'm only jittery because I'm feeling guilty about leaving without telling them. It'll be worth it. We'll get to St Bernards and be home before they know it. They might not even realise we left in the first place.

'I haven't got the Jammy Dodgers,' says Charlie. 'I gave the rest of the pack to that homeless guy at the station just before you ran to the bog.'

That's Charlie. He's a good kid. Even if his brain *is* inside out. I realise now why the homeless man gave me the thumbs up.

'Can I go to the buffet car?' he pleads.

'No chance,' I reply. There's barely anything in my wallet and we've still got to figure out how to pay for somewhere to stay the night. I reach into the rucksack and pull out a squashed sarnie, even though there are still five hours till lunchtime. 'Here. Have this. I made them last night.'

'Ding dong!' he says as he unwraps the cling film and peeks under the top slice of bread. 'My favourite. Ham and jam.'

Yep. That's right. Ham and jam *on the same sandwich*. He

started eating them when he was two. Back then he just liked the way they rhyme, but it turns out they're delicious. Over the last year I've even started eating them myself. When Charlie was little, Dad always used to tease him – *Do you want cheese and fleas next time? How about egg and leg? Chicken with sick in?*

'Can you time me?' says Charlie, dangling the butty in front of his mouth. Charlie loves me to time him doing anything. I start my stopwatch and he shoves the whole thing into his gob. His cheeks are bulging out as his jaws work up and down. Finally he gives a painful-looking swallow then opens his mouth and sticks out his tongue to show there's nothing left. Apart from some globs of liquefied sandwich that is. I stop the watch.

'Seven point two nine seconds,' I say, impressed if a little disgusted.

'Oh yeah! New record!' exclaims Charlie, doing a little bum-wiggle dance in his seat.

I shake my head and tuck into my butty. It tastes *so* good. Sometimes you don't realise how hungry you are till you start eating. When I've finished the first half, I wrap the other bit up and put it back in my bag. I'm saving it for myself, but I'll probably end up giving it to Charlie when he starts moaning again later.

'You still haven't told me why we're going to St Bernards,' he says, picking bits out of his teeth.

I yawn. It's been a long morning. 'Something to do.'

Charlie looks confused. 'But we could do anything.'

'Yeah, but –'

'D'you think we'll see the dolphin?'

I shrug. 'Hope so.' It isn't time to tell him yet, so I close my eyes to show him the conversation is over. The gentle swaying of the carriage is so relaxing that within seconds I feel myself starting to drift and . . .

DOLPHIN

My eyes scanned the harbour to where Charlie was pointing. I couldn't see anything at first. But then I noticed it on the surface of the sea, about fifty metres from where we were standing, darting in between the boats. A glimpse of fin. A hint of arched back. A light grey shadow cutting through the water.

'Oh my life,' I said. 'Is that a shark?'

'Dolphin,' said someone near me, but I didn't turn around to see who it was. My whole body was tingling and I felt like I'd been clamped to the ground.

The dolphin disappeared underwater and we struggled to look for it between the boats. Then, after a few moments, its pointy nose poked up next to an orange buoy. Everyone by the railings cheered and it set off again, slicing through the calm water. After a while it stopped and bobbed up and down, showing off its white chest. Then, with a sudden explosion of spray, it burst up into the air.

Even today I can picture its leap perfectly, almost in slow motion – its body straining as it catapults upwards, showering down droplets of water that catch the sunlight like tiny flecks of gold. The way people gasp as it hangs in the air. The slow, graceful turn of its body. The unexpected smash as it lands back in the water, breaking the spell. The flick of its tail before it shoots forward, out of the harbour and towards the open sea. That feeling of emptiness – grief even – when I slowly realise it's not coming back.

We stood there for ages, not speaking, before I eventually broke the silence. 'Whoa,' I said, puffing out my cheeks. 'Just *whoa*.'

'Amazing,' sighed Mum.

'Don't see them in Preston docks, eh, lads?' said Dad.

I didn't answer. And neither did Charlie. His mouth was hanging open.

SOME WEIRDO ON THE TRAIN

My eyes open with a start. Was I asleep? Everything suddenly seems very different. Agitated and confused, I look around.

A girl is next to me, jabbering away on her mobile phone. She looks Indian, about sixteen, tight jeans, flowery perfume and completely beautiful. I feel embarrassed like I always do when I'm this close to an older girl.

'. . . No, it's not right. I'm not happy . . .'

Her accent's lovely – proper Midlands – *roight . . . oi'm . . .'appay.*

Hang on. *Midlands?* Where are we?

And where's Charlie?

The girl looks at me like I've just crawled out of a pond. 'Do you mind?' she says. *Moind* – amazing. Then she shakes her head and mutters something under her breath.

Suddenly I'm worried.

Where *is* Charlie? And hang on – where's my rucksack? Who's nicked it? No. Not the rucksack. Whatever happens. Not the rucksack. It's got everything in it. I can feel panic squeezing round me like a boa constrictor and I frantically look under the seats, but it's not there so I pull on the girl's sleeve till she yanks it away from me . . .

'It was taking up the seat so I put it on the rack,' she tuts, pointing a sharp pink thumbnail behind her, her hand over the mouthpiece. 'I didn't wanna wake you up. You were . . . drooling.'

How humiliating.

She looks me up and down. With what? Horror? Pity? Then she goes back to her phone call. '. . . no, just some weirdo on the train . . . anyway, tell me about this boy . . .'

Some weirdo on the train. That's me. Five words that stab like little daggers under my ribs. And my brain is being yanked in different directions – the girl, Charlie, the rucksack – and I spin round and scan over the back of the seat at the luggage rack and there's the rucksack like she said, thank God, but where on earth is Charlie? He's not gone. He can't have gone! But he's nowhere to be seen and the panicky feeling keeps growing and this girl's perfume is actually really strong and is it me or is the carriage just a little bit too hot and those lights are prickling my eyes again and . . .

'Tickets, please!'

A conductor's right there next to us and I'm all light-headed and wobbly and I don't know why but I stand up like a proper fool and I hold out the ticket and he stamps it and says we'll be in Birmingham in twenty minutes, which I guess is a good thing but only if I find Charlie, and I feel a bit faint and now the conductor's looking at me and asking if I'm OK, and I can hear my own breath inside my skull, which I guess is just a box of bone with your brain in when you think about it and the girl is staring at me too and she's standing up as well and saying '. . . This guy's proper freakin' me out . . .' and she's looking around for another seat, and the next thing I've barged past her and stumbled through the sliding doors in between the carriages and it's so clattery and rattly in there I've got to escape and get to the toilet and I struggle through the next door and into the loo and slam the door and before I know it there's my chewed-up ham-and-jam sandwich staring up at me from the silver bowl.

My Brother

There was a young fellow called Martin
Who gobbled baked beans by the carton.
They went straight from his tum
Right down to his bum
And now he can't stop himself fartin'.

By Charlie Tompkins
Aged 10

STAGE 3B

WOLVERHAMPTON TO A SHOP AT
BIRMINGHAM NEW STREET STATION

18 MILES

TRAIN AND WALKING

POEMS AND PUKE

I've got serious jelly legs as I step through the automatic door back into our carriage. My hair and face are soaking wet from splashing water on them, and I have to hold the wall for support. I feel totally relieved when I see Charlie sitting there in my seat with the rucksack next to him. He's writing in my notebook, his tongue sticking out of the side of his mouth as he scrawls huge, slow letters across the page. The conductor and the Indian girl have both gone.

'What are you doing?' I say, a bit too harshly, as I grab the notebook off him. We're pulling out of Wolverhampton, which I know is close to Birmingham because we went past a sign for it on our way to Cornwall last year. Through the window I can see the girl walking away along the platform. She doesn't look back, which in a funny way makes me feel better.

'Writing a poem,' he replies. 'Just like you. Hey! I didn't know you write poetry, bruv.'

Saying nothing, I glance at his poem. It's a limerick about me and some beans. I might've found it funny if it wasn't for the panic, the sick and the fact I'm trying to be cross with him for going missing.

'Don't ever disappear like that again,' I say, slipping the notebook back into my bag. 'I thought I'd lost you. Where did you go?'

'I was using me noggin,' he says, tapping the side of his head. 'I could see the conductor coming from right down the train so I crawled onto the luggage rack and hid behind that massive suitcase. Didn't wanna wake you up. I know you get cranky when I do that.'

'Huh,' I say. Charlie's forever waking me up in the middle of the night to ask me some stupid question like, *Why's custard yellow?* Or, *Why don't the Pyramids have any windows?* I usually chuck a pillow at him.

There's a long pause as he studies my face. Finally he asks, 'Are you feeling OK?'

I check that the biscuit tin is still closed before fastening up my rucksack again. 'I'll live.'

Puking up my butty on a train. Not normal. Then again, these are not normal circumstances. I watch through the window as the train crawls past warehouses and factories and retail parks and tower blocks and endless housing estates into the city. I need to sort myself out. In a few minutes I'm going to have to figure out what we do next.

TATTOOS

At Birmingham New Street, the platform's packed. There's a low roof above us like we're underground, and it makes me feel a bit claustrophobic. I hold onto Charlie's shoulder as we shove through the impatient scrum of people trying to get on our train. I'm not sure where we're going and I'm still confused and jittery so I attempt to stand still for a moment. But then we're being jostled by people heading for the exit so we have to push our way through to a bench at the side of the platform.

'What's the plan, boss?' says Charlie as we sit down.

I could really do with that piece of paper with the train times on it. Even though I know it's not in the rucksack, I check one more time. If Mum and Dad find it, they'll know exactly which trains we're on and then . . .

Probably best not to worry about that.

'Pretty sure we get a train to Plymouth next,' I say, flicking through the notebook just in case the train times are tucked in there. 'And I think we've got a while to wait but I can't remember.'

I peer around but I can't see an information screen anywhere. While I'm doing that, Charlie reaches over and closes the notebook so he can see the cover. 'Hang on! I didn't notice the dolphin picture before,' he says. 'It's one of mine! Where did you get it?'

I shrug, a bit embarrassed. 'I cut it out of your pad and stuck it on, then I covered it with plastic. I thought it was pretty cool.'

The notebook was just a plain green school exercise book that Mr Hendrix gave me for jotting down my poems. I'd wanted to jazz it up a bit. Charlie was always drawing pictures of dolphins when we were in St Bernards last year, so it reminds me of the holiday.

'Cheers, bruv. That's well good. I feel like a proper artist.' Charlie grins. Sometimes when he smiles he can't control himself, like the smile's taken over his whole face. Suddenly he clicks his fingers. 'You know what – we should get matching dolphin tattoos in St Bernards.'

I laugh. There's no way anyone would give Charlie a tattoo. He looks about six years old. But I'm fairly tall. *I* might pass for eighteen, I suppose. On a good day. If the tattooist was short-sighted. 'Actually that's not a bad idea . . .' I say. A dolphin tattoo. *Perfect.* I wonder how much it would cost. Maybe I'd get a discount if the tattooist *was* short-sighted.

'Where will you get yours?' he asks. 'I think I'll have mine on my face.'

'Bit of an improvement . . .'

'In fact, no. I'll shave my head, then get my whole body tattooed grey so I *look* like a dolphin.'

'Your *whole* body?' I say.

He genuinely seems to think about this. 'Hmm. Good point. Why wreck something beautiful?'

I snort.

'Maybe I'll leave the rest of my body as it is and just have my willy done to look like a dolphin,' he says.

'Ha! A dolphin?' I laugh. 'More like a tiddler! Or a shrimp.'

At that moment, the PNE fans walk past us along the platform, escorted by the police. I stop laughing immediately. 'We're North End till we die' echoes passionately against the ceiling.

The fat one who grabbed me earlier is at the front, red-faced, neck veins bulging and fists pumping. He's looking straight ahead so he doesn't spot us. But that policewoman from Preston studies me carefully as she passes. There's a moment when I'm frozen on the bench as our eyes meet. Then she sweeps her gaze forward and she's gone.

'Let's go,' I grunt, after she's disappeared up the steps. Sitting still is not a good idea.

DOLPHINWATCH

By the harbour railings, Charlie had become totally hyped up. 'A dolphin. Oh wow! Can you believe it?'

Dad waved his arm out towards the harbour. 'That's why you work hard for your holiday, right?'

He was saying it half to us and half to anyone else who'd listen.

'Spot on, sir. Well said,' said an old chap next to us with a grin. He had bright white hair, an open-neck shirt and skin the colour of walnuts. He pulled a mobile out of his shorts pocket and began tapping away, muttering to himself in his rich, deep voice. '7:25 a.m. – bottlenose dolphin. In the harbour. Ten minutes, then left for open sea. Done.'

When he looked up he smiled, noticing us watching him.

'What are you doing, old-timer?' asked Charlie.

Old-timer. Seriously.

'Sorry,' said Mum. 'So rude, Charlie.'

The old man threw back his head and roared with laughter. 'Not at all. Old-timer. Better than old git, I suppose. And, since you ask so pleasantly, I'm updating Dolphinwatch, my curious little fellow.'

'Dolphinwatch?' said Charlie. 'Whassat when it's in trousers?'

'Just a little local website. It records whale and dolphin sightings along the coast here. A few of us post on it. Keep people informed, you know?'

'Gizza look.'

Charlie pulled the old man's wrist down and began scrolling through the screen. The man didn't seem bothered though. In fact, he shielded the phone from the glare of the sunlight with his free hand so Charlie could see it better.

'This 'un's been here pretty much twice a day for the last month or so,' he said. 'Really friendly old girl she is. Big show-off. Last year we had four in the harbour at once.'

'No way!' said Charlie.

'Way,' said the old-timer, opening his eyes wide to show the white bits.

'So if we come back tomorrow we'll see her again?' asked Charlie.

The old-timer shrugged. 'You might. If she's gonna come, she's usually here bang on high tide. Remember though – it ain't an aquarium, so you can never tell. Have a look on the tide charts to help you. All the best now.'

With a casual wave, he strolled off in his sandals.

Charlie rested his chin on the railings and gazed out at the empty sea. 'See you soon,' he said. I wasn't sure exactly who he was speaking to.

CRIME

The departure screen tells us there's almost an hour till our next train. Charlie needs a drink because his 'mouth's as dry as a lizard's flip-flop', so we go up the escalators and along a wide passageway towards the main part of the station.

'Problem,' I say.

There's a barrier in front of us. You've got to feed your ticket into a machine before it'll let you out, but we've only got one ticket. I consider trying to make it through while holding onto Charlie, but there are ticket inspectors everywhere.

'You wait here and don't move,' I say to Charlie. I don't want to leave him on his own, but I don't have a choice.

'Cool. I'll look after the rucksack.' He grins. 'Wouldn't mind cracking open those biscuits.'

I clutch the rucksack to my chest. Since we've been off the train I've had it on my front so no one can pinch it. 'Definitely not!' I snap.

Charlie takes a step backwards. 'Wow! What's bitten you on the bum?'

'I told you. We're saving them till we get to St Bernards.'

'All right, all right,' he says, his voice high-pitched. 'I heard you the thousandth time. Keep your knickers on.'

I take a deep breath. 'Look. I'm sorry. I'm still a bit . . .' I begin but I don't want to finish. 'I'll get you something nice.'

I squeeze his shoulder and lead him over to the wall. He sits down on the floor, and then I head through the barrier.

You can tell Birmingham's a big city as soon as you step out into the main part of the station; it's massive and bright and completely awesome. Light pours through the high glass arches of the ceiling. There are screens, shops, restaurants and *Charlillions* of people scurrying everywhere and bustling past me. It's a bit scary if I'm honest, but I've got a job to do so I take a deep breath and step forward. Gripping the rucksack even more tightly, I stride towards a shop where the snacks and drinks are in a fridge right by the open doorway.

Most of the drinks are really expensive, and when I check my wallet I've only got eight pounds eighty-three left. I've no idea how that's going to last overnight, especially now I'm going to see if I can afford a tattoo in St Bernards as well. How much do hotels and tattoos even cost?

An idea crosses my mind. A stupid one, I know. There's a security guard at the door, looking gormlessly out across the station. I gulp. This is *so* wrong. I can't. I don't do stuff like that. But, then again . . .

In the end the decision is a surprisingly quick one. *Just do it and do it now*, I tell myself. *Do it for Charlie*. I casually walk along the fridge aisle, pretending to inspect the sandwiches and salads while slowly undoing the zip on my rucksack.

A quick peek around the fridge unit towards the entrance. Security guard yawning. Behind me a lifeless shop assistant is rearranging a basket of bananas.

Now!

As nonchalantly as possible, I stroll back along the aisle, my face saying, *Nope, there's nothing here for me.* When I get back to the drinks at the end, I look over to the security guard one more time. He's checking his watch and stretching his neck left and right before lazily waving at someone across the forecourt. It has to be now. I bite my lip. *I shouldn't. I shouldn't. I shouldn't.*

But I do it anyway.

I reach forward, grab a massive bottle of orange juice then slip it into my bag and zip it up in one motion. Shouldering the bag, I march out as quickly as possible and round the corner away from the shop. I take one last look behind me then

Whack!

I stumble backwards. The rucksack hits the ground.

Oh nuts.

I've walked straight into a bright yellow jacket.

And *even worse*, it's that flipping policewoman again.

I gulp. 'Sorry sorry sorry.'

'Oh, hello,' she says, picking up the rucksack, which sloshes guiltily at her. 'You again?'

I try to say hello back but my voice sticks in my throat. She's not too much taller than me and she's got a warm smile that I didn't notice before. Behind her, the PNE fans are being escorted towards the station exit.

'Rail replacement buses,' she says, nodding her head to point and weighing the rucksack up and down in her hand. 'Engineering works. Pain in the neck. Where are you off to then?'

I want to lie but I can't think of anything. 'St Bernards, Cornwall,' I whisper, staring anxiously at my rucksack as it dangles from her hand. *Don't open it, please.*

Her eyes open wide. 'Wow. Long way. Why are you going there?'

Questions questions.

For what feels like ages, I stand there spluttering, trying to think of something to say. Why *am* I going to St Bernards? What *am* I doing? What's the point in *any* of this?

I'm worried I'm starting to look like a Suspicious Character so, eventually, I blurt out the first thing that comes into my head. 'I want to get a tattoo.'

Oh shut up, you complete idiot.

She looks at me for a moment, like she's trying to figure me out.

I have to fill the silence. 'Best place to get them, St Bernards – fishing village, see, and everyone knows that fishermen have tattoos, and loads of artists live there too so it's bound to look good and . . .'

This is awful. She narrows her eyes at me. Suspicious Character? More like a Total Freak.

Then she sniff-laughs through her nose and shakes her head. 'Very good. Well, gotta go. All the best with the tat – don't get anything you might regret. Oh. And I hope you're old enough.'

My head bobs up and down like a nodding dog.

After handing me the rucksack she pauses for a moment, as though she's about to ask me one more thing. My throat tightens. Then she seems to think better of it and turns around before striding towards the exit.

Does this mean I've got away with it?

I'm not going to hang around to find out. My belly is going crazy, like a washing machine full of milkshake. Quick-sharp, I leg it back to the barrier.

HAPPINESS

Standing on a beach
Sand beneath your feet.
Swashing orange juice
Through your teeth.
Dancing alone
In a crowded room.
Free music playing
Boom chinga boom.
Happiness is easy to find.
But you can lose it in a moment.

By Martin Tompkins
Aged 13

STAGE 4A

BIRMINGHAM NEW STREET TO JUST PAST BRISTOL TEMPLE MEADS

ABOUT 90 MILES

TRAIN

REGGAE

I slip back through the barrier and find Charlie sitting cross-legged on the floor where I left him. His lazy eye is closed, his palms are together like he's praying, and he's making an *ommmmmm* sound.

'Is your belly-button laser getting flat again?' I ask.

Charlie opens his eye. 'Nope. Just trying to figure out the meaning of life and . . . hang on . . .' He shuts his eye again. '*Yep.* Got it.'

'So what is it then?' I snort, as Charlie leaps to his feet and dusts off his hands.

'What's what?'

'The meaning of life.'

'Ah. Well, actually, it turns out it's . . .' he says, leaning in towards me, 'cheese.'

I run my hand through my hair. What's he like? 'The meaning of life is *cheese*?'

'Yep. I was surprised too.' He shrugs. 'Makes sense though, I suppose. Anyway, did you get us a drink?'

I hand him the juice. He glugs it, rinses it through his teeth, then gargles before swallowing. I take a nervous sip and shove the bottle into the rucksack before anyone sees.

The relief at not being caught has been replaced with a suffocating mega-guilty feeling. Honestly, I've never nicked anything before, so this is a really big deal for me. Then I remember the omni-special biscuit tin that I stole from the house. And when you add that to not buying Charlie a ticket for the train, that makes three crimes committed in one day. And maybe kidnap as well. So that's four. Actually, is it illegal to run away from home? What about pretending to be an adult when you're not?

Yikes.

I'm a Serial Offender.

Right away I make a decision. As soon as we get home I'm going to send a card to the shop to say sorry for taking the juice. I'll get hold of some money and Sellotape it inside. Maybe I'll put in a couple of pounds extra and ask them to donate it to charity. This makes me feel better.

We check the screen, find out where the Plymouth train is leaving from and walk along the passageway towards our platform without speaking. A busker is playing slow reggae on a battered acoustic guitar. He's shaking his dreads and singing about lazy days at the beach with the sand beneath his feet. He's pretty good as well, his thumb and long fingers gracefully slapping the strings – *boom-ching boom-ching* – eyes closed and his voice all mellow and distant.

As we get closer, Charlie nods his head and clicks his

fingers. Then he just starts dancing in the middle of the concourse. And not *normal* dancing either. Dancing like he's having a fit or something. Flinging his arms and legs around, waggling his head with his tongue hanging out, attempting to do headspins and the caterpillar.

It's pretty funny in a Charlie kind of way, because he's totally out of time with the slow rhythm and he's so uncoordinated – kind of like a drunk baby donkey being electrocuted. Plus no one takes any notice of him, which makes it even funnier. People are just stepping round him the way people seem to do in big cities – staring dead ahead or down at their phones – and the busker's eyes are still closed so he can't see him either. But now Charlie is completely wigging out, leaping up and down and headbanging.

I'm about to start laughing when I hear a 'Hey you!' from behind me.

My heart freezes.

Two policemen are jogging down the concourse, ten metres away and getting closer. Tight short-sleeved shirts. Big muscles. Angry faces.

Oh no.

They know about the orange juice.

I'm a wanted man.

I grab Charlie but there isn't time to move cos the police are closing in on us and I shut my eyes and squeeze him and that shaky feeling is growing inside me again and I make a whining noise and wait for the handcuffs but –

'You know you need permission to play music here . . .' growls one of the police officers.

'Come on, mate. Hop it,' says the other. 'This is twice today.'

I open my eyes and they've got their broad backs to me, crowding the busker towards the wall. I feel relieved for a minute, but then I see the busker's face and I feel sorry for him. His frown seems to show anger, confusion, fear and disappointment all at once.

'Leave it out, man,' begs the busker in a strong Brummie accent. 'Haven't you got any criminals to catch?'

Trying to stay dignified, he stuffs his guitar into its case then pockets the coins from his woolly hat.

'Don't get cheeky with me, son,' snaps the first policeman. 'I could nick you for breach of peace.'

The busker sucks his teeth as he balances the hat on top of his dreads. 'Police,' he says, with every ounce of hate in his body. 'All I'm doing's making people happy.'

'Well, you can make us happy by going home,' says the second policeman, easing him along the gangway by his shoulder.

As they pass, I catch the busker's eye and give him a thumbs up to say I liked the music. He returns it with a sad smile. 'See that?' I hear him say to the policemen. 'People enjoy my music. The world needs more joy and you're stealing it. You're nothing but happiness thieves, man.'

TOILETS AND TICKETS

The Plymouth train is completely crammed. There are people standing in the aisle, and suitcases and bikes everywhere. I manage to find a window seat on a table of four. Straight away I find out that beggars can't be choosers.

On my table are the following people:

– an old woman diagonally opposite me who cleans her false teeth with a little brush and a cup of water before sticking them back onto her gums. Then she picks up the cup of water and swirls it round. It's all cloudy with bits of food floating in it. Finally – *and I promise this isn't a lie* – she downs it in one. Gross.

– an enormously fat, sweaty man next to me. His bare arms are touching my bare arms and I can't escape. He's watching a funny film on his iPad with his earphones in. I only know it's a comedy because he keeps laughing really loudly, his whole body shaking up and down. Sometimes after a big laugh he turns to me, eyes streaming, and shakes his head as if to say, *Wasn't that brilliant?* How should I know, mate? I can't hear it.

– the angriest-looking girl I've ever seen. She has a huge rucksack on her knees, blue hair, multicoloured woollen coat even in this warm weather, pierced eyebrow and lip, and a *come on, I dare you to look at me* glare burning on her face. She's sitting right opposite me in the other window seat and I'm really doing my best not to catch her eye.

Charlie, by the way, is in the bogs. As the train pulled out of Birmingham the announcer said they'd just got a new conductor on board so they'd be checking every ticket. Charlie was actually delighted when I told him to hide in the loo and not to move until I came for him. Told you: he loves a good toilet.

I keep thinking about the busker. He's given me an idea for a poem so I start jotting it in the notebook. But it's hard to concentrate because of the wheezy fat laughter, and the clicking false teeth, and Angry Girl who's trying to read what I'm writing. I glance up at her and she gives me a proper death stare, so I cover the book and finish as quickly as I can.

Mr Hendrix told me to find a cool, calm, peaceful spot to write poetry. This train is definitely not what he had in mind so I don't think the poem's up to much. I mean, it starts out OK, but I end up rhyming *room* with *boom chinga boom*, which is completely lame (and in any case I'm not sure a station concourse is classed as a room). Also, I rush the last line a bit so it ends up having a sad ending.

I know Mr Hendrix would be like, *Hey – don't sweat it. The best poems are always the true poems. Nothing else matters.* But was this poem true? Why did I need that weird last line? I suppose it's because of how the police just stopped the music like that. I wish Charlie was here – he'd have come up with something funnier.

Actually, scrap that. I'm way better off with Charlie in the toilet. By now he would've said something inappropriate about the fat man, or tried to tickle Angry Girl, or asked the old woman if he could borrow her false teeth or something.

Thinking about Charlie wearing the old bird's falsers makes me smile to myself.

'*What?*' snaps Angry Girl.

'Nothing,' I mutter, and I lean back into my chair and close my eyes. This is going to be a long journey.

CLASSIC ECONOMY BUDGET

After the dolphin had disappeared we headed off to find a cafe. All of us were in a brilliant mood and of course Charlie was the most excited of all of us.

'Did you see it?' he was saying, his eyes wide and the words shooting out like sparks. 'The way it just flipped up like that, I've never seen anything like it, I mean it was just *alive*, you know?'

'Course it was alive.' Dad laughed. 'I doubt a dead one'd swim quite so fast.'

Mum gave him a soft slap on the shoulder. '*I* know what you mean, Charlie. But just don't get too excited. You know what the doctors say.'

Charlie's meant to avoid getting overstimulated, just in case his heart beats too fast. Even though he's had millions of tests and scans and check-ups, the doctors still aren't sure exactly how strong his heart is. *It's impossible to tell. He could live till he's a hundred, or, well . . .*

I probably shouldn't think about it really. I mean, Charlie never does.

Charlie waved his hand at Mum like he was batting away her words. 'But it was the most mega-magic thing I've ever seen!' He grinned, practically bouncing up and down. 'It was like a . . . a . . . a bobble hat full of hope and happiness.'

'A *what*?!' cried Dad, as we stopped outside a place called the Sandy Bottom Beach Diner. 'Well, *I'm* wearing a baseball cap full of hunger. Let's all go in here, calm down and get some bacon and a brew . . .'

Inside, we each had a full English breakfast; apart from Charlie, who ordered three fried eggs on top of a bowl of porridge, just to see if they'd make it for him. They did as well, and we were all treated to the sight of it sloshing round his mouth as he relived every millisecond of the dolphin's appearance again and again.

When Charlie had finished his breakfast, which according to him 'tasted of the future', he made us all eat up then dragged us down to the harbour to see if the dolphin had come back. Unfortunately the tide was heading out by then. The fishing boats that'd been bobbing around an hour or so ago were lying tilted in the shallow water, and the harbour walls were slick with seaweed. Of course the dolphin was long gone.

Charlie stared out to sea for a while, quietly scanning the horizon. There was no sign of a fin or even a splash. Disappointed, he made Dad take a photo of a blackboard with all the tide times for the week on it so we'd know when to come back. As we walked away towards the car, he kept glancing over his shoulder as though he expected the dolphin to come slithering up onto the sand any second. It didn't.

For the twenty-minute drive out of town, Charlie was pretty quiet for a change. He sucked his thumb as we whizzed out through the suburbs then along narrow country lanes. In fact he didn't perk up till we pulled into the holiday park. There was a massive sign as we drove in: '*Surfside – One Life – Anything's Possible*'.

'I like that,' Charlie remarked as Dad parked outside reception.

While Mum nipped out to collect the keys, Dad turned round in his seat to face us. 'Right lads,' he said, 'I'll warn you: the caravan might not be the nicest one in the park . . .'

From the brochure we had at home, I already knew that Surfside was a pretty massive site that backed onto a beach about seven miles along the coast from the main town of St Bernards. As well as a pool, a cabaret bar and a games room, it had around six hundred caravans and chalets of all different shapes and sizes. There was some sweet brand-spanking-new accommodation, but we'd booked a 'Classic Economy Budget' caravan, which is a fancy way of saying *Old, Cheap and a Bit Rubbish*.

Dad stroked his stubble and cleared his throat. 'We needed to save a bit of money so we could do more stuff while we're here,' he said apologetically. 'Better to sleep in a cave and live like a king than sleep in a palace and live like a tramp, right?'

I got the feeling he'd been working on this line for a while. 'We really don't mind,' I said, shrugging. I mean, a holiday's a holiday, isn't it? I didn't care where we were staying; I had this quiet, buzzing excited feeling in my belly and I couldn't wait to get unpacked and get the holiday started properly.

But Charlie was staring at the big Surfside sign. 'I'm going to help Mum,' he announced. Then he hopped out of the car and ran over to reception.

They were gone for ages. Dad sat in the front, resting his head on the steering wheel, and I stayed in the back, eating some warm, squashed leftover Starburst from the night before. After about ten minutes they came back to the car. Charlie had a big grin on his face and Mum was looking a bit confused.

Closing the door, she handed a map of the park to Dad. 'They've drawn a circle round where we're staying,' she said. 'We're in Red Zone, right by the sand dunes.'

Dad stared at it for a moment. 'Hang on. That's not right. We should be in Brown Zone. It says here that Red Zone is for Deluxe Premium Sea-View Chalets.'

I raised one eyebrow. 'Deluxe Premium' is a fancy way of saying *Ultra-Posh Super-Expensive*. I glanced over at Charlie, who was deliberately looking out of the window.

Mum shook her head. 'I know. We got upgraded.'

'Upgraded?!' cried Dad, 'Well, you can just go back in there and *downgrade* us. I'm not paying another five hundred quid for a fancy kitchen and a nice view.'

Mum put her hand on his arm. 'No. You don't understand, love. It's free.'

'You what?'

Still looking out of the window, Charlie said casually, 'I just asked if they had any spare. Turns out they did.'

'They aren't fully booked this week,' explained Mum, 'And they've had some cancellations so they had quite a few empty. They said they wouldn't normally do it, of course, but Charlie charmed them . . .'

'Don't ask, don't get,' said Charlie.

Dad spun round to face him. 'What? And they just gave one to you, like that? For nothing?'

Charlie looked at him with his head tilted to one side. 'Well, I had to sing to 'em first.'

'He's not kidding either,' said Mum. 'They were like, "How can we refuse after hearing that?"'

I felt a giggle tickling my throat. 'What did you sing?'

'"If I Was a Rich Man",' Charlie said, totally deadpan.

'Were you any good?'

Mum shook her head. 'Absolutely. Bloody. Awful. I think they only upgraded us to shut him up.'

There was a moment's silence before we all creased up laughing.

Charlie didn't laugh though. He just smiled. 'Anything's possible,' he said to himself. 'Anything's possible.'

FAT MEN AND TOILETS

Along with most of the other people on the train, the fat man finally gets off at Bristol. *Relief*. His heavy metal T-shirt (for a band called Monkey Apocalypse) clings to his body along with a kind of musty, damp odour. Charlie would've said the smell was the mould growing under his man boobs.

The old woman gets off too. She's spent pretty much a whole hour eating a single salmon sandwich with tiny sparrow bites. It was gross – her false teeth clacking up and down, and her mouth full of mushed-up fishy paste. Why did she bother cleaning her teeth if she was just going to eat a butty straight after?

Anyway, when she stands up, the fat man grunts, 'Hurry up, Mum,' and I realise that they're together. This is really weird – they haven't said two words to each other the whole way. In fact, they haven't even looked at each other.

I suddenly think of my mum. *We* don't really chat much these days either. I really hope I don't end up like the fat man when Mum's old – lost in another world and totally ignoring her.

Oooh, he'll miss her when she's gone. That's what Mum would say if she was here. I just know it.

I feel my stomach sag. I hated being near them but, somehow, the idea of the old woman dying and the fat man missing her makes me feel sad. I make a mental note to chat to Mum more after I get back tomorrow. You shouldn't take people for granted.

Mum.

Is she out of bed yet? Has she realised we've gone? Is she bothered? Has she noticed the missing biscuit tin?

The last one makes me smile sadly to myself and I tap my rucksack to make sure the tin's still there. It is.

Hmm. Maybe I should just send her a text to let her know we're OK. I reach for my phone but then I remember it's still in my open drawer at home, which in turn makes me regret making it so obvious that we'd run away. I wish I could go back in time and tidy up after myself – alarm off, drawer shut, cereal box away, train times in my rucksack, lid back on that jar.

It's too late to do anything about all that now though. I can't go back and change anything. I have to look forward. As for Mum, I'll get in touch once we've done everything we need to do in St Bernards.

Thinking of families, I remember that Charlie's been in the loo since Birmingham. As the train pulls out of the station, I pick up the rucksack and wander down to him. The aisle is empty now and it feels weird, walking in the opposite direction to the way we're going. Am I going backwards or forwards or just standing still? I knock on the door and there's a swooshing noise as it slides open. Charlie's sitting on the loo seat, looking surprisingly happy.

'Has the conductor been round yet?' he says, jabbing the *close and lock* button.

I let him have a big glug of the stolen orange juice, then drink some myself. 'No. The train's been too busy. I reckon he'll be along soon. I'll come and get you soon as he's gone.'

'No rush,' he grins, waving his arms around to show the space. 'I've got the best seat in the house. Look at this legroom.'

'But it stinks,' I say, then tuck the juice bottle back into my bag.

Charlie shrugs. 'I'm used to it. I've been sitting next to you all morning, remember. Anyway. I'm starving. Can I have a biscuit now?'

'I told you,' I say, rolling my eyes, 'when we get there. Now shift out the way. I need to use the facilities.'

As I – ahem, you know – *go*, Charlie's jabbering in my ear the whole time. It's a wonder I don't get stage-fright.

'Hey, do you remember the bathroom in the chalet at Surfside? It was like a palace.'

I smile at the memory. 'And it was the only room we could get a phone signal,' I say over my shoulder.

'Yes!' Charlie chuckles. 'I'd forgotten that. I spent hours

in there, checking Dolphinwatch on Dad's phone.'

'Mum said if you stayed there any longer someone'd use you as a bog brush!'

Charlie laughs so much he has to take a blast on his inhaler. Mum's got a cracking sense of humour when she's in the mood, you know. I guess that's just Charlie's influence – he brings out the best in everyone.

Then Charlie's face turns serious. 'So . . . since going to St Bernards was your idea, have you been checking it then?'

'Checking what?' I say, zipping my trousers up then turning round.

'Dolphinwatch.'

I wash my hands and dry them under the pathetic air dryer. 'Course I have. Every day since last year. You know that.'

Checking Dolphinwatch was something I got in the habit of doing after the holiday had finished. It's a bit strange that it's me who does this, I suppose – I mean, it was Charlie who was into looking at it when we were actually *in* St Bernards. But he gets bored easily, and I just felt like carrying on once we'd got home.

When I turn to face him, his eye is wide open. '*And* . . . ?'

I try to look innocent. 'And what?'

'Is it back?' he asks, half pleading now.

'Is what back?' I say, playfully flicking water at his face. I'm determined to drag this out as long as I possibly can.

'The dolphin, you muppet!' snaps Charlie. 'Has it been coming to the harbour or not?'

'Maybe,' I say. I ruffle his hair and wink as I slip back out into the carriage.

SAND DUNE

A Shape Poem

my
brain's
a sand dune,
thoughts like tiny
jumbled grains of sand
piled up into a hairy mountain.
And sometimes the weight of it becomes
too great so that one of the grains slips and tumbles,
dislodging others and dragging them downwards in a chaotic
swirling mini-avalanche that briefly changes the shape of everything,
until later, when a gentle gust of wind eases across the dune, filling the holes
and smoothing out the drifts until the dune is reshaped and peaceful once again.

By Martin Tompkins
Aged 13

STAGE 4B

SOMEWHERE JUST PAST BRISTOL TO AN ALLEYWAY

DOWN THE SIDE OF A CHEAP HOTEL IN EXETER

VIA EXETER ST DAVID'S STATION

ABOUT 80 MILES, PLUS AROUND 300 METRES

TRAIN AND SPRINTING

KICK IN THE SHINS

I'm feeling pretty pleased with myself as I saunter back down the train. I bet Charlie's going nuts in the toilet right now.

Ever since we left the house this morning I've been waiting for the right moment to let him know about the dolphin. According to Dolphinwatch, it disappeared during the autumn and winter, then it came and went through the spring and summer. But it's been back every day for the last few weeks so the time's right for us to go. High tide's at seven this evening. We'll get in at five-ish so we should have plenty of time. Of course the ocean's not an aquarium, but still, I just *know* the dolphin's going to be there.

The happy feeling doesn't last long. As I slip back into my seat, I realise that Angry Girl is reading my poetry book. She's folded the page right back and she's just reading it like she owns it. I must've forgotten to put it back in my bag. *What an idiot.* Without thinking, I snatch it off her.

She raises her eyebrows in surprise then fixes me with this strange look that I can't quite understand. Her dark lips are pursed and she's gazing hard at me. Is she mad at me for taking back my own book? Or is she poking fun at my poems?

Either way, I decide to ignore her and look out of the window. I don't feel bad about grabbing the book off her. The poems are mine. No one else is allowed to read them apart from Mr Hendrix. What made her think she had the right? Immediately the train shoots into a tunnel. The noise and the sudden darkness make me jerk my head away from the glass. Angry girl smiles, which doesn't suit her face. Why are some people such idiots?

There's a light kick on my shin. I move my leg to the side but she does it again.

'You all right?' she asks.

I shrug.

'Interesting poems.'

I don't answer.

'Where you going?' It feels more like a challenge than a question.

Still I say nothing. The pressure from being underground rises in my ears.

Another kick when we burst into sunshine again. 'Come on. Tell me. Where you going all alone?'

I can't place her accent – a bit posh? A bit Devon? And her face and voice are so unreadable that I can't tell if she's making fun of me. For the first time I properly look at her. I reckon she's about seventeen, but she's small and thin so she could easily be three years older or three years younger. She'd be pretty if it wasn't for the mad coat and the stupid blue hair and the aggressive eye make-up, not to mention the angry expression.

OK, so there are quite a few barriers to her being in any way fanciable. Not that looking good is all that counts. I mean, a *personality* is just as important as being beautiful. Unfortunately it seems like she might be lacking in that department as well.

This time she boots me really hard. 'Don't be rude, answer the question.'

Rude? I think reading someone's private notebook then kicking them is a bit ruder than ignoring them.

'St Bernards,' I say, doing my best not to wince. Hopefully she'll leave me alone now.

'Cornwall? Oooh, very nice,' she trills. 'Might go there myself.'

'Oh. Right.' *Like I honestly care.*

'Wanna see something?'

Not really, I think. I'm just about to ask her to go and bother someone else when she loosens her rucksack and pulls out a large plastic bottle, which she dumps on the table with a thud. 'Pretty cool, eh?'

The plastic isn't see-through, so I can't tell what's inside. Grinning smugly, Angry Girl spins the bottle round and points to the label. A few of the words jump out at me:

PARAFFIN. CAUTION. HIGHLY FLAMMABLE.

She clicks her fingers and, as if by magic, a lighter appears in her hand. 'Imagine,' she says, licking her lips and slowly turning the flint with her thumb. 'One spark from this and *KABOOM!* No more train.'

My head is light and I feel like I'm looking down on the carriage from a long way up. I don't like it. Not one little bit.

Angry Girl slides it proudly back into her bag. She looks delighted to have scared the pants off me. 'So you'd better be nice.'

There's something really unsettling about the way she says this – almost friendly and almost threatening – and the way she stares at me for a little bit too long afterwards.

What is she? A pyromaniac? A terrorist? *I've got to get away.*

Grabbing my rucksack, and making sure I've got my poetry book this time, I wobble nervously to my feet and stumble down the aisle. I want to change carriages, but then I realise I'm heading the wrong way. This is the front of the train. There's nowhere else to go. Just a locked door and a sign telling me not to distract the driver.

Oh God.

I turn around. She's still in her seat. At least she hasn't chased me yet. But I'm not going past her again. No way. I look around. Think. *Think.* I could pull the EMERGENCY lever but it says there's a fine of £250 for improper use. Would this be improper use? I don't know. But I *do* know I haven't got two hundred and fifty quid.

Maybe I'll tell the conductor when he comes along and only use the emergency brake if she follows me. *Good idea.*

Take it easy. She hasn't moved yet. I flop into the sideways-facing seats that are near the exit doors. Once I've sat down, I take several deep breaths and try to keep it together. I'm about ten rows away from her, I reckon, and if I stand up I can just about see her. Unfortunately Charlie's toilet is down the other end of the carriage. I figure out a plan. At the next stop, I'll get off, sprint along the platform and get back on again further down the train. Then I'll hide in the toilet with him till we reach Plymouth.

This plan relaxes me a bit. Eventually I feel brave enough to see what Angry Girl's up to, so I peer over at her. The way that she's looking out of the window, all moody again, makes me think she might not be about to follow me. I'm all right for now. As long as I stay calm that is.

It's OK, I tell myself. *Write a poem. That'll help. No, even better,* read *your old poems. You won't get carried away then – you can keep one eye on her.*

The book automatically falls open on the third or fourth page, which must be where she'd folded it back. It's one of my first poems from last year – right from when I started poetry club. It's a pretty weird one all about a sand dune. Only it's not about a sand dune. It's about my brain. I remember that I didn't want to show it to Mr Hendrix at the time. As soon as I'd finished it, I'd slammed the notebook shut. He just said, *No problem – I understand. Sometimes the poems you write reveal something that catches you by surprise.* When I finally allowed him to read it a few weeks ago, he patted me on the back, then flicked ahead to my more recent stuff and said, *Look how far you've come.*

Personally I didn't think the sand-dune poem was all that bad. But still, that doesn't mean I wanted Angry Girl to read it.

HAIRY MOUNTAINS

When we drove round to it, the chalet didn't disappoint. It was a beautiful log cabin nestled among pine trees. Inside was even better – an airy open-plan kitchen and living area, two bathrooms and three bedrooms (even though Charlie said he preferred to share with me). There were leather sofas, a great big telly, a sound system with a dock for your iPod or phone, and even an Xbox.

But that wasn't the best thing.

The whole back wall of the lounge was made up of these super-swish patio doors that kind of folded back on themselves. Through them was a wooden balcony with a table and chairs and our very own barbecue.

'Oh wow!' exclaimed Charlie, leaning over the balcony railings. 'Hairy mountains.'

'They're sand dunes,' I said, rolling my eyes.

Topped with spiky green grass, the dunes stretched in a ragged line across the back of the row of chalets. The balcony was perfectly placed so you could see the ocean framed between two of them.

'It's gorgeous,' whispered Mum, joining us on the balcony.

'You should sing more often, son,' said Dad.

But Charlie didn't reply. He was already climbing over the railings. 'Race you to the top!' he called to me, dropping from the side of the balcony and landing on the sand three feet below.

'Careful!' Mum said, but he was off. 'Go after him, Martin. Make sure he's OK.'

Doing as I was told, I followed him. Charlie was halfway up the dune by the time I got to the bottom, but I soon overtook him, my feet sinking into the fine sand. I collapsed at the top. My thighs and lungs were burning but I hardly noticed. I was looking out on the most amazing sight – a huge arc of golden sand curling off for miles in both directions. Hundreds of people were sunbathing, playing on the beach, or surfing and body-boarding through the huge white breakers. Over to the left, the harbour and white cottages of St Bernards poked out from behind a rocky outcrop, tiny and hazy in the distance.

'Check that out!' I gasped, but when I turned round, Charlie still hadn't joined me. He was lying on his back two-thirds of the way up the dune, wheezing and spluttering.

'You OK?' I said, sliding down on my backside to meet him.

'In-ha-ler,' he wheezed, clutching his throat and jabbing his thumb towards the chalet. His eyes were round with panic and his face was bright red.

'Oh nuts!' I exclaimed, and I half ran, half tumbled down the dune to get help.

POEMS AND ANNOUNCEMENTS

It takes a long time before I convince myself that Angry Girl isn't going to blow the train up. For a while she looks out of the window, occasionally flicking her eyes towards me. Then she takes out a book, shoves her rucksack up on the shelf above and starts reading. Amazingly, she even manages to read angrily, flipping the pages over like she's trying to hurt them. I'm relieved her paraffin is out of reach and I feel myself starting to relax.

Soon, the conductor comes along from the back of the train and asks for her ticket. I hear Angry Girl say something that sounds like, '*Non capisco Inglese.*' It could be Spanish or Italian but it might be total gobbledygook. She's frowning at the conductor like she's no idea what he's talking about. The conductor repeats himself slowly and tries to draw a ticket in the air.

'*Non capisco,*' she says again, shaking her head apologetically and sounding out every syllable. '*Mi dispiace. Sono una straniera.*'

'I said. Ticket. Now. Or no travel. Understand?' the conductor says.

He's beginning to lose patience with her, but she seems not to notice and just nods happily back at him. I notice that this is the first time she hasn't looked angry. '*Grazie mille, signore.*'

With this he gives up. As he walks along the carriage towards me, he tells her over his shoulder that she'll be getting off at the next station. Angry Girl blows him a kiss.

She's clearly a total nutter! And an armed one at that. I should definitely tell the conductor about how she threatened to blow up the train. And how she's only pretending to be foreign. As I'm handing him my ticket, I say, 'Excuse me,' but at that moment his phone rings.

'Sorry, gotta take this,' he says, giving me back the ticket without looking at it before bustling his way back along the train talking into his phone. 'Remember. Off next stop,' he says to Angry Girl as he passes, putting his hand over the receiver.

'*Ti amo anche,*' Angry Girl calls after him.

I take a deep breath, put my notebook back in the rucksack and slip it onto the floor for safekeeping. *Everything's OK. She'll be off soon, and then I won't need to worry.*

An announcement over the tannoy breaks into my thoughts. 'Ladies and gentlemen, we will shortly be arriving at Exeter St David's,' says the crackly voice, which I recognise as the conductor's. 'If there's a Martin Tompkins from Preston on board, please would you make yourself known to the police at this station.'

I freeze.

The police!

Why do they want me?

Is it about the orange juice?

Or has Mum called them?

Whatever. This is not good.

As the train slows, Angry Girl saunters down the carriage in my direction, rucksack over one shoulder. I catch her eye, which feels like a mistake. She must notice the panic on my face and I can tell that she's realised it was *my* name that was announced.

As she passes, she leans in towards me and whispers, 'Quick tip. Try not to look so obvious. Don't let them know who you are.'

As the train begins to creep into the station I'm still trying to figure out if she's actually being kind. The platform we're stopping at is on the other side of the train from my seat. Two police officers – a man and a woman – are standing there, watching the train come in and talking to a guard. There's a dull, heavy feeling deep in my gut as we inch past them. Ignoring Angry Girl's advice, I scramble across the aisle to get a better look. Finally we squeak to a stop.

For ages the train doors don't open. Have they stayed locked for a reason? From somewhere down the train I can hear someone jabbing at the button then swearing when it doesn't work. Pressing my face against the window, I can just about get the angle to see back along the platform. Our conductor has stepped off the train and has joined the police officers and the guard. They're about thirty metres away, level with the middle of the train.

The policewoman shows the conductor a piece of paper. He squints at it, rubs his chin then wags his finger towards my carriage. The police officers follow him along the platform. I want to run, but there are a couple of people in the aisle.

Stay calm. Don't let them know who you are.

I sit, frozen, trying and failing to look casual. My eyes follow the conductor and the police as they walk along the platform and past my window. Now they're at the doors right next to me. The conductor takes out a kind of T-shaped key, plugs it into the side of the train then turns it. There's a clunk-hiss as all the doors on the train open at once. I can see that the piece of paper in the policewoman's hand is a photo. *A photo of me?*

It's too late. They know exactly who I am.

I don't have time to think. The people trying to get off are shuffling awkwardly to one side so the conductor and the police can squeeze past.

All except Angry Girl that is.

'*Ciao, bello,*' she says, placing her hands on the conductor's chest.

'Not again . . .' he moans.

'Excuse us, please,' calls the policeman from behind him.

But Angry Girl refuses to budge. As the conductor tries to shift her out of the way, she turns to me. 'Go on then!' she urges, yanking me out of my seat with her free hand. 'Leg it!'

In a split-second I've made my decision and I'm wriggling out of the seat and back along the train, away from the police and past a couple of people in the aisle and there's an old guy in front of me putting on his coat but I manage to shimmy round him while the police are calling behind me but they struggle to get past Angry Girl and I'm in the clear along the aisle and out through the next set of doors, barging off the train past the people trying to get on and I have a quick pause on the platform to find the exit sign then I'm up over the footbridge two stairs at a time with my feet slapping the ground and down the other side and someone's yelling for me to STOP NOW and another guard has a puzzled glance at me as I run past but before she can react I'm out of the station sprinting past a line of taxis, looking over my shoulder but there's nobody following, and I turn left then right then right again and the next thing I know I'm leaning against a wall down the side of a hotel, retching and gasping and trying to catch my breath.

It's only then I realise I haven't got the rucksack. And I haven't got Charlie.

LOST

A Chant

Lost in a strange town
I sat and cried
Cos I realised I'd lost you
And lost something inside.

Repeat again and again

By Martin Tompkins
Aged 13

STAGE 4C

THE ALLEY BY THE SIDE OF A CHEAP HOTEL IN EXETER TO THE WORST CAR IN THE WORLD

8 METRES

WALKING

PAINS AND MEMORY LOSS

I don't know how long I've been here, squatting against the wall and rocking backwards and forwards.

The only thing I *do* know is that when I realised about Charlie and the rucksack I spun out big time – maybe the second-worst one ever – and it felt like my brain was spurting out all over the place like lava from a volcano. I must've been screaming or something because I remember that someone (an old woman?) came down the alley to see what was up, but I waved her away, howling like an animal. In my head I can just about picture her terrified expression, but whenever I think about it, her skin peels off, her eyes turn dark red like a zombie's and she begins clawing at my face. I know this didn't happen. I think it's just my brain going wacko again because it can't deal with the trauma.

A few minutes go by.

I'm feeling exhausted from the panic attack. It's been ages since I've had one. I should've known it was on the way – what with the mini-meltdown at Preston and the puking on the train and just the *stress* of everything – but it's still hit me hard and fast like a ninja.

At least they always pass. Even the bad ones. And now I'm starting to come back to the real world again, aware of the sharp bricks against my back, and the aching thirst in my throat, and the raw throbbing of my knuckles. I wish I had that bottle of orange juice. The thought of it makes me lick my lips.

I notice a thumping pain in my head, and when I open my eyes I have to squint against the dim sunlight of the alleyway. There's an overflowing wheelie bin opposite me and I'm surrounded by a really strong stink of toilets. When I look at my knuckles I see they're shredded and bleeding, and I can't really bend my fingers. Maybe I punched the wall like I did that other time this happened. Who knows?

For a few minutes, as I slowly come round, I flicker in and out of awareness. Behind the hum of traffic noise I can hear trains pulling in and out of the station and suddenly I'm flying above my train as it rattles through the countryside, then I'm zipping into the carriage through an open window. And there's the rucksack, under the seat where I left it. And I float down the carriage, past the handful of bored passengers and into the toilet, where I can see Charlie. He's happy and unaware that anything's wrong and I want to hug him, but when I reach for him he disappears like he's made of mist and I'm back here in the smelly alleyway before I know it.

I feel sick about Charlie. *What kind of a brother . . . ?* I know

I was panicking, but come on – there's no way I should've left him behind. How can you lose a person? I'm not even meant to be here in the first place. And now there's no way I can get to him, or the rucksack. *The rucksack as well.* How stupid can I get?

This is a real disaster. I was only trying to do the right thing, but it's all collapsed. *What have I done?* My shoulders shake, I press my knuckles into my eyes and I begin to sob.

SURPRISES AND PHONE CALLS

As I cry and cry a rhyme starts to form in my mind. It's about being lost, but I can't get past the first few lines – they're on an endless loop like there's no way out of my problems. Charlie's lost. The rucksack is lost. I'm lost. In more ways than one.

Gradually I become aware of someone else here. Dunno how – I didn't notice any footsteps. It's just that feeling of being watched. I steel myself. Is it the police? I guess I'll have to hand myself in. I don't have the stomach to run again. And they might get Charlie and the rucksack back for me. But then I'll have to go home and I'll have to answer to Mum and Dad. The whole trip will've been a waste of time.

I move my hand away from my eyes and feel my body jolt. Of all the people in the world, it's Angry Girl who's squatting in front of me, holding a bottle of water out towards my face.

'Have you taken something?' she says. Her voice is much softer than before.

I gulp. 'A bottle of orange juice. From a shop in Birmingham station,' I croak. 'But I'm gonna send them the money, I promise.'

After a few seconds I realise she means *drugs*. Just being asked this question makes me feel weird and I don't like it. Not-So-Angry-Any-More-Girl cracks up, but not in a nasty way. I'm surprised how concerned she looks, even when she's laughing at me.

I take a glug from the bottle. Then she pours some of it onto my knuckles and dabs them gently with a tissue.

'Why were the pigs after you?' she asks finally.

I've only been back in the real world for a minute so I have to shake a weird picture of giant pigs chasing me down the train out of my head. 'Ran away from home,' I say finally, wincing from my stinging fingers. I can bend them so at least they're not broken. 'Me and my brother.'

She stands up and looks around, adjusting her massive rucksack. I'm surprised at how this news doesn't surprise her, if that makes sense. 'Parent trouble?'

'Sort of,' I say.

'Huh,' she says, nodding. 'Tell me about it. Bit young for running away though, aren't you?'

'We're only going for a night.'

'Fair enough. Make them sit up and notice. Long as you stay safe though. It ain't as much fun as you might think. Where's he gone then?'

'He's hiding in the toilet on the train,' I say. Suddenly I'm gripped by an urge to *do* something. 'I've got to get back on the train to meet him. And I need to get my bag.'

I stand up way too quickly and get a massive head rush

that makes me stagger back against the wall. Angry Girl grabs me by the shoulders and looks at me through her heavy eyelashes. 'You're not going anywhere. I was watching you just now, from the street. You were totally freaking out. I dunno what all that was about, but the train's long gone and *you* need to take it easy for a while. Anyway, you go back to the station and who d'you think'll be waiting for you?'

'You don't understand,' I say, brushing her hands away. 'The bag's really important. I can't lose it. I *can't*. And Charlie needs me. And it's all my fault and –'

I try to push past her but she stands in my way. 'Is your brother thick?'

Her question stops me. 'No.'

'Then he'll stay on the train till Plymouth and wait there till you show up, won't he?'

'Well, maybe,' I say. I suppose it makes sense – he knows that's where we're heading. And I remember Dad telling us once – if you get lost on the way somewhere, wait at the destination. You need rules like that when you've got a liability like Charlie running about. But then again . . . 'What if he heard the announcement on the train and he got off here too? He could be wandering round the station looking for me right now. He'll be lost and alone and he needs me.'

Angry Girl weighs this up. 'All right. I can go look for him in a minute. But we should do something about your bag if it means so much to you.' She pulls out her phone. 'What kind is it?'

I describe it to her while she's doing a search on her phone. Then she taps the screen and holds the phone to her ear. 'Ooh, hello there, dear,' she says, after it's rung a few times. The sudden change in her accent is amazing – she sounds just like an old Scottish lady. 'Is that the Plymouth station manager? You'll no' believe it – I've made a silly wee mistake and left my rucksack on the train at Bristol . . .'

After Angry Girl's arranged for my rucksack to be taken off the train by a member of staff at Plymouth, and for it to be collected from the station by her grand-daughter (giving a perfect description of herself by the way), she hangs up.

'Sorted,' she says, pleased with herself. When I look confused she explains: 'If I'd said it was yours, they mightn't have given it to me. The police are looking for a lanky kid who got off at Exeter, not a *wee old Scottish wifie who hopped off at Bristol*, remember.'

Even when she's putting on the accent again, she still sounds seriously businesslike. The way my brain's buzzing, it feels nice to have someone who can take charge, even if I don't really know who she is, or whether I can trust her.

'But how are we gonna get to Plymouth?' I ask, which is just one of the millions of things that are making my brain ache right now.

Angry Girl smiles. 'You let me worry about that. Now, I need to know what your brother looks like.'

ANYTHING'S NOT POSSIBLE

By the time I'd legged it back to the chalet, Dad was already vaulting over the balcony rail, holding Charlie's inhaler, while Mum climbed down behind him. We sprinted back up the dune together and stuffed the inhaler into Charlie's hand. He took a few blasts of it before his breathing slowly returned to normal.

Dad rubbed his back. 'You've got to be more careful, son. You know you can't go running off like that without your puffer.'

Mum was nervously rubbing the little gold crucifix she wears round her neck between her finger and thumb. 'Oh God, I thought –'

Face like thunder, Charlie ducked away from her hand and stumbled angrily down the sand dune on his own. Halfway down he turned round. 'It's a stupid crappy lie!' he shouted.

'What are y—' began Mum.

'The sign!' snapped Charlie. 'Anything's *not* possible! Just when you think . . .'

His voice trailed away and he stormed off again. After

struggling to pull himself up the balcony railings a few times, he stomped away and disappeared round the side of the chalet. A few seconds later, we heard the front door slam.

I wanted to go after him but Dad said to let him calm down and the three of us sat on the soft sand together for a while, not saying anything.

Eventually we followed him back. Inside the chalet, the toilet door was locked and Dad's phone had gone from where he'd left it on the kitchen table. It was weird how quickly things had changed: the excitement of seeing the dolphin, the buzz of the chalet, the panic of Charlie's asthma attack, and now this.

For the next hour the toilet door stayed closed. The rest of us unpacked and wandered about, barely talking to each other. Charlie's mood was like a blanket over a parrot's cage, subduing and silencing all of us. After a while, Dad nipped off to the shop to get milk, but I didn't fancy going with him. I was desperate to be out on the beach. Bored, I switched on the Xbox, but I couldn't get into it so I chucked the controller down on the sofa and marched over to the bathroom. I'd had enough.

THE WORST CAR I'VE EVER SEEN

When Angry Girl comes back twenty minutes later, I don't realise it's her at first. This is because she's in the passenger seat of a car that pulls up at the end of the alleyway.

'No sign of anyone who could be your brother,' she calls, rolling down the window, 'so hurry up. We need to get a move on!'

I tentatively walk over. This is honestly the worst car I've ever seen. It's an ancient VW Polo. The passenger door and bonnet are red, but the rest of the car is a kind of dirty cream, except for the huge rusty holes at the bottom of the bodywork. And the massive permanent-marker picture of a skull and crossbones on the roof that looks like it was done by a hyperactive four-year-old.

The driver is a youngish guy with no top on. He's skinny, with loads of tattoos all over him. His head is shaved and he's wearing those dinner-plate earrings that stretch out his ear lobes. I'll be honest – I'm terrified of him. But then he leans forward in front of Angry Girl and gives me a toothy smile. 'Hear you need a lift, squire,' he says in a proper friendly Devon accent. 'Hop on in.'

My hand reaches out for the rear door handle. Then I stop. What am I doing? I don't know this weird man with the dangly ear lobes. I don't even know Angry Girl. This whole thing's making me nervous.

'Don't wanna hurry you, old boy,' says Dangly Lobes, 'but I'm on a double yellow and I ain't rich enough to pay parking tickets.'

'We want to get your brother, don't we?' says Angry Girl, and I don't know why but I trust her. I know it's wrong and stupid and against every sensible bit of advice you could ever be given, but what choice do I have? Charlie and the rucksack are gone. I can't go back to the station and I'm completely skint. I can't get the rucksack back without Angry Girl to collect it for me from Plymouth and I can't get to Plymouth without climbing into Dangly Lobes' car. It's not like I've got any other options. But still, I don't move.

Angry Girl hops out and stands really close to me. Her voice is low and secretive. 'Look. Your poem. The one about the sand dune. It was . . .' She blows a strand of hair out of her face. 'It was like . . . reading about *myself*. Like you'd been inside my head or something . . .' She pauses to swallow. 'When you were having trouble with the police I just had to help you, and then, when I saw you in the alleyway, well . . .'

Still unsure, I look at her for a few moments. It's not too long ago that I thought she was going to blow me up.

She seems to know what I'm thinking. 'I'm sorry about

when we were on the train. Sometimes I find it –' she frowns, like it's a real struggle to push the words out – 'hard to be nice.'

The look she gives me then is so surprisingly kind and unguarded that I find myself biting my lip and climbing into the car.

NOT

That funny-looking kid's not weird or stupid,
He's just different.
And this pen isn't a pen,
It's a key that opens up hidden doors.
And that dolphin isn't a dolphin,
It's a magic creature that changes people.
I guess what I'm trying to say,
Is what you think and what things actually are
Can be two very different things.

By Martin Tompkins
Aged 13

RUBBISH!

STAGE 4D

THE ALLEY BY THE SIDE OF A CHEAP HOTEL
IN EXETER TO PLYMOUTH STATION

45 MILES

CAR

CAKES AND OLD PEOPLE

During the first fifteen minutes of the car journey from Exeter to Plymouth, I learn the following things:

– Angry Girl is actually called Henrietta but I should call her Hen because 'Henrietta's the kind of name you give to a canal boat'.

– Her dad – who she's not seen since she was seven – is Italian, which is why she was speaking Italian to the conductor on the train. (She tells me that at one point she actually told the conductor that she loved him!) She never buys a train ticket and this is her favourite way of not getting busted for it.

– Dangly Lobes is actually called Wesley, although most people call him Doctor Lizard for reasons that aren't really clear.

– Doctor Lizard (Lizard for short) is Hen's best friend and he'll do anything she asks, although they are definitely not boyfriend and girlfriend. They grew up near each other in Exeter and like hanging out and going to music festivals together. Whenever she's in town she sleeps in the spare room at his parents' house.

– Lizard's car is called 'The Tank'. I thought the outside was bad, but the inside is even worse. There's no carpet and that rusty hole in the floor is so big I can see the road under my feet. The seat is scarred with deep gouges, like it's been attacked by a panther. Black smoke pours out of the exhaust the whole time, and the engine rattles, shakes and whines as though it's in pain.

– Lizard works as a carer in an old people's home. This doesn't seem to fit with his crazy image but, after a few minutes of knowing him, he seems to be a very nice person.

– According to Hen, the old people at the home love him. In fact, when he got sacked for teaching a seventy-eight-year-old woman with two false hips to skateboard, the rest of the pensioners refused to eat until he got his job back. When he returned to work, Lizard celebrated by baking scones for all the residents. Henrietta says that Lizard is *amazing* at baking. This is another thing I wasn't expecting to learn about him.

As soon as Hen mentions the baking, Lizard tells me to fish out a tin from behind his seat. I reach down and open it up. It's filled with delicately decorated fairy cakes with swirly blue icing and silver balls sprinkled on the top.

'Made a batch for one of the old boys. It was his ninety-second birthday,' he says, smiling at me in the rear-view mirror. 'These are the leftovers. Help yourself.'

They look utterly awesome, but it's funny: he'd be the last person in the whole world you'd expect to have made them.

This just shows you shouldn't judge people by how they look. It reminds me of a poem I wrote once about how we see things. I didn't like it at the time so I crossed it all out and scrawled 'RUBBISH!' across the page. But it makes sense now, I guess. Mr Hendrix wouldn't let me tear the page out of my notebook. He said that poetry's about emotion, and the scribbling shows I was frustrated and angry at the time so it's actually kind of cool to leave it as it is. I like Mr Hendrix.

'I keep telling him to go on that *Bake Off* on the TV,' says Hen, but Lizard grins and shakes his head.

I take a cake and quickly hand the tin over to Hen. I don't want to hold onto it for too long because it makes me think of the omni-special-leftover-from-Christmas biscuits in my rucksack, which in turn make me think of Charlie.

I bite my lip but, strangely enough, I don't freak out again. I think this is for three reasons. Firstly, no matter how bad the car might be, I know that we're moving towards Charlie. Hen was right: my brother might be a looney tune but he's definitely not thick. I know he'll be waiting for me when I get there. I just know it.

Secondly, I'm a lot less stressed after what happened in the alleyway. Like I wrote in the sand-dune poem, everything seems calmer when the avalanche is over. In fact, I feel a bit floaty.

And thirdly, well, the cake is utterly delicious and there aren't many situations that can't be improved by a delicious cake, right?

'Why d'you need to go to Plymouth then, fella?' says Lizard, steering the car with his wrists and unwrapping his cupcake at the same time. We're way out of Exeter now on open moorland – bleak and empty. There's a part of me that thinks this would be a perfect place for two weirdos to bring a stranger they've just kidnapped so they can murder him, but I shove this thought down before it takes over.

'Told you on the phone, he's lost his brother. And he needs his bag,' says Hen. She snatches the cake out of Lizard's hands, unwraps it for him then shoves it into his open mouth so that he can steer properly.

Lizard chews the cake and swallows but doesn't say anything.

I fold up my cake wrapper and shove it in my pocket. Of course this is pointless – the car is littered with old takeaway wrappers and drinks cans – but I don't feel right dropping rubbish when he's doing me such a massive favour.

'Thanks for taking me,' I say. 'I appreciate you going out of your way.'

''S all right,' replies Lizard, picking his teeth. 'Hen rings me up out the blue and says, *Take me to Plymouth, boy.* I'm only working mornings this week so I says, *All right, why not go on a bit of a mission, eh? I'll pop in and see my nan while I'm there.* No bother to me if you hop in too. More the merrier, I say.'

I feel myself frowning. This doesn't make any sense. If Hen had wanted to go to Plymouth in the first place, why didn't she stay on the train? That's where it was heading after all.

She'd have got there way quicker if she hadn't got off. OK, I know the conductor had told her off for not having a ticket but she didn't exactly look scared of him. And in any case, on the train she'd said she *might* go to St Bernards.

'I didn't know you were going to Plymouth too,' I say to Hen.

'Just decided when we got off the train,' she replies. 'Was gonna stick around in Exeter for a few days but –'

Lizard interrupts her. 'Did your mum know you were passing through town?'

'Drop it, Wesley,' she says, running her hand through her hair. I notice the way she uses his real name. The atmosphere in the car suddenly feels tense.

'Well. Just saying. I saw her in the shop last week and she said she ain't seen you in four months and dun't know if you're alive or –'

'I said drop it,' she snaps.

'Ooh,' says Lizard, mockingly. 'Someone's tired.'

Hen shakes her head and half laughs. 'You're an idiot.'

'You just *suddenly decided* to go to Plymouth?' I say, blurting out the question before I can stop myself. The post-panic-attack wooziness seems to stop me from holding things in.

'Oh, didn't she tell you?' says Lizard cheerfully, 'Bit of a wild one, our Hen.'

'Stop it,' says Hen, but her voice is playful now, not angry.

'All set to go to art college last year, then what does she

do? Quits school just before her exams.'

'Went off it,' mutters Hen. 'Don't like being tied down.'

Lizard taps the steering wheel. 'You can say that again. Goes where the wind takes her. Then shows up back here whenever she fancies it.'

Hen sniffs. 'Nothing wrong with seeing a bit of the world. And anyway, if I stay in one place too long the police get to know my face. And that isn't what I want, trust me.'

I gulp. Why doesn't she want the police to know her? *Is* she a terrorist? Or a murderer? What the hell am I doing in this car with her? The feeling that this was a bad idea comes flooding back. The speedometer is jiggling at about fifty miles an hour. For a moment I try and figure out what will happen to my body if I open the door and dive out.

Lizard glances up at the mirror and seems to notice my worried expression. 'Ha. Don't worry, boy. She ain't a gangster. She's a *juggler*.'

'A juggler?' I say.

Hen squirms in her seat, too embarrassed to answer me, so Lizard speaks for her. His voice is super-enthusiastic. 'Oh yeah. Best I've ever seen. Rocks up in a town. Juggles away. Draws in a crowd. Few coins in the hat. Then does one before the coppers catch her. Dunno why they don't like her, mind. Dun't do any 'arm, far as I can see.'

'You need permission to do anything,' mutters Hen, 'and they don't like anyone different.'

'Tell you what though,' continues Lizard, slapping the

steering wheel for emphasis, 'you should see her with them fire sticks. Cor – she proper gives me the fears, man. I swear she'll go up in flames one day.'

'It's paraffin,' she says, matter-of-factly. 'Doesn't burn too hot. Looks worse than it is. Sorry for scaring you with it on the train by the way. Just trying to break the ice.'

A *juggler*. Of course. What a relief! I laugh to myself. I feel a bit foolish for thinking she was going to blow up the train.

I try and relax, and look out of the window at the moorland. I'm starting to feel like maybe everything might turn out OK . . .

DOLPHIN AND CHIPS

'Oi!' I said, banging on the bathroom door. No answer. Mum told me to let him be but I wasn't having it. 'Stop ruining our holiday and get out here. You promised Dad – being miserable wasn't an option, remember?'

'Leave me alone,' replied Charlie.

I took a deep breath.

'Aw, come on,' I begged. 'We're meant to be having fun. Look. We'll do whatever you want.'

I didn't know if this was true or not but I had to try something.

'Anything?' he replied finally.

I looked over at Mum who was putting tins away in the kitchen cupboards. She nodded. 'Yes,' I said.

The toilet door opened slowly. Charlie was standing there with Dad's mobile phone in his hand and a sly grin across his face. I smiled. He was back. 'What do you want to do then?'

'Fish and chips for tea,' he said cheerfully, as though nothing had just happened. 'Back in St Bernards. The seafront. Seven o'clock tonight.'

'Is that it?'

He nodded.

'And you promise to stop spoiling everyone's fun?'

He saluted solemnly. 'Brownie's honour.'

For the rest of the afternoon we went to the site's outdoor pool, which was pretty sweet. It had slides and inflatables, and me and Dad played volleyball with a family from Wales. Charlie didn't join in – Mum thought he should rest after his asthma attack. At first he was a bit fed up about this, but Mum bought him a pad from the site shop and he sat at a plastic table and drew pictures of dolphins, which seemed to keep him entertained. When I got out I told him they were amazing, even though they had that scruffy, babyish look that all Charlie's pictures have. Charlie grinned, proper chuffed. It's rare for him to sit still for that long.

At exactly twenty past six (Charlie was determined we leave on time) we piled back into the car and drove into St Bernards. Dad got the hump cos he didn't want to drive again, but Mum told him we'd promised Charlie and that was that. He soon cheered up though because Charlie was back to his excitable best, firing out jokes like torpedoes the whole way there: 'Did you hear the one about the man with five willies? *No.* His underpants fit him like a glove.'

And so on and so on.

When we got to St Bernards, Dad and I went to the chippy while Mum and Charlie went to find a bench. It was crowded in the shop and all along the prom – the evening was warm and clear, and it seemed everyone in town had had the same idea. Finally we got to the front of the queue, grabbed four trays of chips and a couple of fish to share (a complete rip-off, according to Dad) and wandered along the front to find Mum and Charlie.

The tide was in again. Out at sea, the sun was beginning to set and a rippling golden path stretched across the water from the harbour wall to the horizon. The air was sharp with seawater and vinegar.

When we found Mum and Charlie, they weren't on a bench. Charlie was standing on the bottom rung of the railings, with Mum next to him. They were part of a group of people staring out to sea.

'It's back!' Charlie was bouncing up and down. 'I knew it would be back and it is! Look!'

As if he'd called it over, the dolphin cut through the water right in front of us, skirting the harbour wall right by our feet. Up close it was even more beautiful – a grey shadow ringed by a glistening halo of water.

'Yes!' cheered Charlie, leaning right out between the bars. 'Yes! Yes! Yes!'

Mum had to pull him back by the jumper. 'Calm down, Charlie. I don't want you having another attack.'

So we stood by the railings, eating our chips and watching the dolphin as it glided round and round the bay, sometimes dipping down for a few minutes then popping up somewhere else, sometimes hissing out a cloud of spray as it eased past.

It was amazing how much happiness it gave people – everyone was clapping and hollering as it passed them.

Once it stopped just ten metres in front of us, its head nodding up and down, a wide smile and sharp little teeth visible over the gentle waves, a crackling, squeaking noise coming from its throat.

'Oh wow! Oh wow! It's looking right at me!' cried Charlie. And then, without warning, he grabbed Dad's portion of battered cod and threw it into the sea. It landed with a splash and sank under the water. The dolphin ducked its head and followed it down.

'Ha ha! Go on, lad!' Charlie cheered.

Dad was furious. 'What d'you do that for?'

'Steady,' said Mum.

'That's four quid's worth of fish, that,' protested Dad. 'I hadn't even had a bite.'

'The dolphin looked hungry,' said Charlie to Dad. 'Here – have you got any tomato ketchup to go with it? He might be a fussy eater.'

Mum and I tried not to giggle.

'I'll turn you into tomato ketchup if you're not careful,' said Dad, but he said it in a kind of not-so-mad-any-more way that made Charlie smile. 'Right. Finish your chips and let's get back. I fancy a beer from the fridge.'

'Awww,' begged Charlie. 'Just ten more minutes.'

'No,' said Dad firmly.

But Charlie refused to move. In fact we ended up staying

for nearly an hour. Even though we all loved watching the dolphin, Mum, Dad and I got a bit bored after a while. Plus it was getting darker and cooler, and by quarter past eight we were all shivering and we could barely even see the dolphin any more.

In the end Dad had to prise Charlie's fingers off the railings and drag him away. Even then, Charlie made him promise that we'd come back at least once a day for the rest of the holiday to see the dolphin again.

And we did.

DROP-OFF AND SEARCH

There's a line of buses outside Plymouth station (more rail replacement services, I guess), so Lizard drops us off as close as he can and says he'll do a spin round the block and see if he can find somewhere to park.

I thank him and climb out. Hen looks around and takes off her multicoloured coat. 'Put it on,' she says to me. 'The police can email your photo to every station in the country if they want. Doesn't take much to confuse them though. Trust me.'

Even though it's really warm for September, I do as she says and follow her over to the station entrance. She walks quickly, making me keep a gap between us. As I follow, I wonder what made her quit school and start juggling for a living, running about the country, dodging the police and never seeing her mum. And I wonder why she pretends to be so angry when she's actually really nice and kind.

We reach the entrance, which is a pretty dreary place – a low 1970s building next to a big tower block. It's even more depressing when I see that Charlie isn't waiting for me outside. But then I think it through – why *would* he be here? He'll be expecting me to come in by train so he'll be on the platform. I know it.

The inside of the station is surprisingly well done out, with white tiles on the floor and these cool sail-shaped things underneath the glass roof. It's quiet and there's still no sign of Charlie. Luckily I can't see any police either.

'Go and wait over there. There's a chance that this is a set-up and they know it's your bag. If you see any coppers, leg it, all right?' says Hen, steering me towards a rack of tourist leaflets. I flick through one about an aquarium, but really I'm peering over the top of it for Charlie.

A couple of minutes later Hen comes back. She hands me my rucksack. I check inside – the biscuit tin is still there, which is awesome beyond words. The bottom of the bag's a bit damp and sticky so I guess the juice has leaked, but that doesn't matter. 'Thank you so much!' I say.

'No worries,' she replies. Her phone beeps and she reads the screen. 'Lizard. He's parked somewhere he shouldn't be so he's not gonna stick around. I'll run and get my stuff from his car. You find your brother. I'll meet you on the platform and we'll sort out a plan.'

I tell her to thank Lizard for me as she darts out of the station. But as soon as she's gone I start to feel uneasy. What did she mean by a *plan*, exactly? I thought she'd help me to get the bag and Charlie and then we'd go our separate ways.

Hmm. I'll figure this out once I've found my brother.

There's a bored-looking guard standing by the ticket barrier. 'Excuse me. What platform did the last train from Birmingham come in on?' I say, as confidently as I can.

She frowns. For a moment I think she must know who I am, but then she says, 'Platform six, love.'

I feed my ticket into the machine and sprint up the stairs, along the footbridge and follow the sign down to platforms five and six. There are a few people dotted about the platforms, reading papers, drinking coffee and messing about with their phones, but I can't see Charlie anywhere.

Just as I'm starting to feel worried, I notice a bench right at the far end of the platform. There's a small boy sitting there. Confused face. Scruffy hair. Baggy jumper. Thick glasses. Peppa Pig eye patch.

'Charlie!' I shout.

He looks up and gazes around. I call again and wave my arms like crazy, and eventually he peers towards me. A grin slowly spreads across his face.

MY BROTHER CHARLIE

A Kenning

Tiny fighter
Cot biter
Inn keeper
Dreadful sleeper
Walrus flopper
Trump dropper
Chalet upgrader
Biscuit-tin raider
Sandwich rhymer
Dune climber
Patch wearer
Bedroom sharer
Asthmatic wheezer
Little geezer
Dolphin watcher
Now I've gotcha!

By Martin Tompkins
Aged 13

STAGE 5

PLYMOUTH TO SOMEWHERE ELSE

NOT SURE HOW MANY MILES

TRAIN

HUGS AND ROLOS

I sprint along the platform and dive onto Charlie, giving him the biggest rib-crushing hug ever.

'Gerroff!' he says, but he's laughing his head off and I don't want to let him go ever.

There are tears running down my cheeks and I'm digging my nails into his shoulders, hugging him tighter and tighter. I'm crying like a baby but I honestly don't think I've ever been so happy in my life. 'I'm sorry,' I say. 'I'm so, so sorry.'

'That's nice,' he croaks, 'but I think my lung's just collapsed.'

Snuffling and giggling at the same time, I let him go, slap him on both shoulders and have a look at him. 'I'm so glad you're OK.'

'Where did you disappear to?' he asks. 'I looked everywhere for you. I've been sat here like a lonely penguin.'

'Didn't you hear the announcement on the train about the police?' I said. 'It's been . . .'

I can't finish the sentence though because I'm crying again and I've got to cover my eyes and clench my teeth together for a few moments.

'No, I didn't,' he says. Then there's a pause and his eyes sparkle with excitement. 'The police? *Ace!* Are we wanted men?'

I swallow and take a deep breath, then wipe my face with my sleeve. 'Sort of. But it's fine. I think. I had to run away and I was in such a rush that I forgot you and the bag and I'm so sorry, honestly . . .'

I'm about to cry again but Charlie waves his hand. 'Forget it. What was it you were saying in the train toilet about the dolphin? Is it really back?'

'Yes!' I say. 'It's back, and we're going to see it. I promise.'

'I knew it!' exclaims Charlie, clenching his fists and shaking them excitedly. 'We should celebrate. Look at this – I found a couple of Rolos on the train when I came out of the loo. Bit squashed and warm – like someone had been sitting on them – but still . . . amazing what people throw away. Fancy one?'

He holds them up to me. They're flat as pancakes and they're not even wrapped. *Gross!* I shake my head. Charlie shrugs then chucks them both into his mouth.

'Cool coat, by the way,' he says, the Rolos slopping about in his cakehole. 'Did you rob a charity shop? Is that why the fuzz are after you? And, *hey*, what happened to your hands?'

'I borrowed the coat from a friend. And I had an argument with a wall,' I say, but the mention of the police makes me uneasy. 'We should get moving. The next station we need's called St Something-or-Other.'

'St Something-or-Other,' he says, pushing his specs up his nose. A trickle of Rolo-juice dribbles out of the corner of his mouth. 'Is that near Who-Knows-Where-Ville?'

'There'll be a timetable somewhere – I'll know the place when I see it written down,' I say, thinking yet again about the piece of paper in my room with the train times on it. 'It's about two hours away, I think. We change trains there and it's about another ten minutes after that. Not long now, I promise.'

'And then we'll get to St Bernards?' he says.

'Yep.'

'And then we'll see the dolphin?'

I look up at the station clock – five to three – and bite my lip. 'Hope so.'

'And then I can have one of the omni-special-leftover-from-Christmas biscuits.'

'We'll see.'

At that moment there's a shout from across the tracks. 'Martin!'

I look over. At first I tense up in case it's the policewoman, but then I see Hen. She's standing opposite us on the next platform.

Charlie's face hardens and he narrows his eyes suspiciously. 'Who's *that*?'

'Hen,' I reply, waving over to her.

'I'll come over!' she calls, pointing towards the stairs. But our view of her is blocked by a long, streamlined intercity train that rolls slowly up to our platform.

'I don't like her,' says Charlie.

'Eh?' I reply, totally surprised. 'But you don't know her. Trust me, she'll grow on you. She helped me get the bag back. And she got me a lift. I wouldn't have found you if it wasn't for her.'

The train squeaks to a stop and a door clunks open right in front of us.

'Don't care. Come on,' says Charlie, dragging me towards the train by the hand. 'We're getting out of here.'

I stand my ground. 'What are you talking about?' I say, confused. This isn't like Charlie at all. 'She's our friend.'

Charlie stares angrily at me. 'No, she's not. Let's go. Now. She'll just get in the way.' He releases my hand and storms onto the train.

'This is mental,' I call after him. 'You don't even know where it's going.'

But Charlie is already sitting down in the carriage and the train doors are beeping like they're about to close. I look along the platform. I can see Hen's feet as she jogs down the stairs. Now her shins. Now her legs.

The doors hiss at the exact moment that Hen reaches the platform.

I feel like a horrible person, but I can't afford to lose Charlie again. Turning away from Hen and hoping she doesn't see me, I dive through the doors just before they close.

HOOKED

'You can tell a good holiday,' said Dad, 'cos everyone's got a big smile on their face.'

He was right. The holiday was *amazing*. After that first day, we didn't stop beaming the whole week. On Sunday and Tuesday we went to the beach. I tried bodyboarding and Charlie buried Dad in the sand, while Mum sat and read her book. Monday we went to Land's End, then we played crazy golf back at the site till it got dark. Wednesday was a theme park (where Dad and I went on a roller coaster and Charlie managed to lose a shoe on the teacups ride) followed by an utterly brilliant Monster Truck Extravaganza in a park outside St Bernards.

Somehow, along with all of that, Charlie still managed to get down to the harbour at least once every day to watch the dolphin. Dolphinwatch and the tide timetable ruled everything: a stop-off in St Bernards on the way to or from somewhere; a quick nip out in the car at lunchtime for Mum and Charlie, while Dad and I played in the sea or had a kick-around back at the site.

Charlie was happiest at those times. He'd stand, mesmerised, watching the dolphin skim around the harbour for as long as we'd let him. Sometimes he'd be pressed against the railings, sometimes drawing or taking photos with Mum's camera, sometimes chatting to the old-timer from Saturday. But always there'd be a massive grin plastered across his face.

On top of that, Charlie spent hours learning about dolphins – finding out facts on the internet on Dad's phone, drawing pictures of them in his little pad. He even made us go to the local library so he could read books about them.

Yep, the dolphin had changed him all right. Mum said she'd never seen him concentrate for so long. As the week went on, even his drawing and colouring-in improved – instead of his usual messy, multicoloured scribble, he'd take his time, carefully sketching then following the lines with his felt-tips.

Everything was perfect.

Until Thursday.

It was a wet day and we'd been to visit an old tin mine, which was a lot more fun than it sounds – creeping about deep underground in the dark. Once Dad hid in this little alcove and jumped out on us, but Mum told him off and said he'd do Charlie a mischief if he wasn't careful. While we were in the museum afterwards, Charlie suddenly announced it was time to go. High tide was at four o'clock and we'd promised.

At the harbour in St Bernards, sheets of drizzle were shrouding half the bay. To be honest, the rest of us were a bit bored with the dolphin now, so we huddled under a shelter by the side of the lighthouse with a flask of tea while Charlie paced up and down the railings in front of us, peering through the rain.

After fifteen minutes of us watching Charlie watching the sea, there was still no sign of the dolphin. Dad called out to him: 'Come on, son! It's chuckin' it down. You've seen one big fish, you've seen 'em all.'

Without turning round, Charlie replied that actually dolphins are mammals. He was starting to look agitated now and he shoved twenty pence into a telescope. Ten seconds later, he stepped off the little platform again, muttering about how useless it was.

'Well, what did that old fella say the other day? It's the ocean, not a zoo,' said Dad.

'Aquarium,' muttered Charlie, still looking out to sea. 'And anyway, it should be here. It's high tide.'

'Maybe it's the weather?' suggested Mum.

'It's a dolphin,' Charlie said sarcastically, turning round at last. 'It lives in water. It's not gonna be scared of a drop of rain, is it? Do you think it's gonna look out the window and say, *Ooh, I'm staying indoors. I haven't got an umbrella and a freaking anorak*?'

'All right, sorry, Mr Grumpy,' said Mum, her eyebrows raised. 'No need to get cross.'

'Well, don't be so thick then,' he snapped.

'Oi!' growled Dad. 'Cut it out.'

This was totally out of character for Charlie. The only times I'd ever seen him like this before were when he'd been frustrated he couldn't do something.

We sat there in awkward silence for another ten minutes, Charlie pushing more coins into the little telescope till he ran out of money. Eventually, with the rain soaking him to the bone, we peeled him away and dragged him back to the car.

On our way past a small office on the seafront, Charlie picked up a leaflet for a boat tour offering 'Incredible four-hour sea-fari around the coast' and handed it to Dad.

Dad rubbed the back of his neck, then tucked the leaflet into his back pocket. 'Well. Er. We'll see, eh, son?'

That evening, while the rest of us had a monster game of Cluedo, Charlie sat in the corner, drawing his dolphins and eating Haribo. In fact he hardly said two words all evening.

Later, in bed, he finally talked to me. 'I wonder where she was,' he said through the darkness. The dolphin was always a *she* – I guess because the old-timer had said so on Saturday.

'She'll probably show up tomorrow,' I said.

'Maybe Dad'll take us on that boat trip,' said Charlie, his voice hopeful and excited. 'They do 'em from the harbour. The old-timer said yesterday it's the best way to get up close to wildlife.'

Dad had left the leaflet on the kitchen table. At twenty-five quid for adults and fifteen for children, I seriously doubted we could afford it. 'Wouldn't it be great if you had a pet dolphin in a tank?' I said, trying to change the subject. 'You know, then you could see it every day.'

The bedside light flicked on. Charlie doesn't wear his glasses or patch in bed, so his face always looks strange, but tonight he had an expression I'd never seen before – total disgust. 'You really don't understand, do you?' he said. His voice was cold.

'Understand what?' I asked, confused.

But Charlie just grunted angrily and switched off the light. Then I heard him flop back to bed, his covers rustling as he turned away to face the wall.

I lay there, staring into the darkness. I had no idea what I'd said wrong.

HIDING AND ESCAPING

I sit facing Charlie at a table. This train is well smart – all plush dark seats, clean carpets and tinted windows. But I can't enjoy it because we've been sitting here for two minutes and we still haven't set off from the station. I can see Hen from my window, wandering about on the platform, looking for us. After a while she pauses, confused. There's an awful pounding in my brain. I don't want to breathe. *Why isn't the train moving yet?*

Then there's a loudspeaker announcement: '*We're sorry for the delay; we're waiting for a goods train to pass through the station ahead of us, so sit back and relax and we'll be moving shortly.*' The cheerfulness of the voice irritates me, like it's giving me good news. We *need* to get away from here before Hen sees us.

I grind my teeth together. On the platform, Hen is running her fingers through her blue hair. Then suddenly her head tilts to one side and she approaches our train, peering in through the next window to ours. Oh God. She's only a couple of metres away. Charlie and I duck under the table so we're hidden. *Why won't this train just get a move on?*

'This is really mean,' I say. 'After everything she's done for us. I shouldn't have listened to you.'

'Rubbish,' says Charlie, his face flat against the wall. 'We don't want her interfering with our business, do we? Other people are trouble. You think she cares about the dolphin? What if she makes us late?'

'You're the one jumping on a random train,' I say, but Charlie just shrugs.

I peer over the table. Hen is moving along the platform away from us now. Part of me feels relieved, but this is still horrible. It's like someone's got hold of my guts in their fist and they're trying to rip them out. I suddenly find myself cross at Charlie. The way he's acting reminds me of the holiday, when he didn't seem to care about anything else but the dolphin. While we were there I sometimes wished he'd never seen it.

'*You and your stupid dolphin,*' I hiss, surprised at how angry my voice sounds. I can't remember the last time I got mad at him. An old woman across the aisle is staring at me, and Charlie's face is a mixture of shock and fear. I take a deep breath and lower my voice. 'I'm sorry.'

'Still not nice though,' he replies, and I know he's right. I'm only being like this because I feel bad about Hen. I huff out my cheeks and I'm about to say sorry again but I don't, because, for the second time that day, I've got that feeling of being watched. And when I turn to my right, there's Hen, glaring in at me through the window.

EMPTINESS

By Martin Tompkins
Aged 13

STAGE 5

(ADJUSTED AND CLARIFIED)

PLYMOUTH TO PAR (BY FLUKE)

36 MILES

TRAIN

HURT AND EMPTY

I can't stand to catch Hen's eye. Behind the heavy make-up she looks so *hurt*, so let down. 'What are you *doing*?' she mouths at me, her forehead all creased around her eyebrow piercing.

I feel my mouth wobbling, trying to find words, but nothing comes out.

Hen slaps the window with both hands and storms away towards the door. And now she's repeatedly jabbing the button. Luckily the door doesn't open.

When will this flipping train get out of here?

That stupid cheerful voice again: '*Ladies and gentlemen, we apologise again for this delay. Teas and coffees are available . . .*'

I feel like screaming that I don't care about the teas and coffees. I just want to get away from here so that I won't feel so terrible any more. But now Hen's back at the window.

'Sorry,' I mouth at her, but she's already turned her back and she's prowling off down the platform.

I sit back in the seat, head in my hands. There's a part of

me that's surprised I'm not having another meltdown. I guess that maybe the one in the alleyway was like taking the lid of a shaken-up bottle of Coke. Everything fizzed out and there's nothing left now.

'Good riddance,' says Charlie, dusting his palms together, and it takes everything in my body not to whack him one.

Fuming silently, I grab the notebook and pen from my bag and try to come up with a poem. But I can't write anything beyond the title so I start drawing a dot on the page. Then I make it bigger, pressing harder and harder till the nib tears through the paper and you can see the lines on the page below. The poem was going to be called 'Emptiness', because that's how I'm feeling right now. Mr Hendrix would probably look at the dot and the hole and say, *Great job. That looks like a pretty good picture of emptiness to me.* But this isn't much consolation.

I feel so stupid. All I can think of is how this was such a terrible idea. The entire trip. I should've known Charlie would end up being like this. I wanted it to be magical. I wanted him to enjoy it. But something about that dolphin just makes him become so single-minded and unpredictable.

RESCUE

The next day, when I woke up for breakfast, Charlie was already checking Dolphinwatch on Dad's phone.

'There's something wrong,' he said, before I'd even had a time to say good morning. 'She's still not been back.'

'It's eight in the morning,' I yawned. 'Give her a chance.'

But Charlie kept tapping the screen to update it, which was totally pointless.

Dad strolled in and clapped his hands together. 'Right, lads! Get dressed. We're out all day. Big surprise.'

'We're going on a boat trip?' asked Charlie, bouncing up and down.

'Definitely not,' said Dad. 'I've had enough staring out to sea to last a lifetime.'

Charlie dumped the phone onto the sofa and screwed up his face like a baby. 'Aw.'

Dad ignored him. 'We're going to the zoo!'

'Cool!' I said. I love a good zoo.

'But what about the dolphin?' cried Charlie, 'It's not been back to the harbour, and if we went out on a boat then –'

'We weighed up the cost of the boat trip, love,' said Mum kindly, 'and it was just too expensive. We got an online discount for the zoo. They've even got a penguin pool. It'll be just the same.'

This was the wrong thing to say.

'No. It. Won't!' cried Charlie, stamping his feet. 'And what about high tide? We'll miss it. It's this afternoon at th—'

'Look, son,' said Dad, mildly irritated, 'I've already bought the tickets, and we're not wasting another minute at that harbour.'

Wasting? mouthed Charlie.

'We'll go tomorrow morning, Charlie,' said Mum, appearing at Dad's shoulder. 'Before we go home. Promise.'

'But . . .' said Dad.

Mum squeezed his arm and gave him a look that said, *Don't argue.* Dad sighed.

So off we went to Newquay Zoo. It took ages to get there because of the traffic, and it seemed like even longer cos Charlie was sulking all the way. Then, just as we arrived, Dad got a text from his service provider asking him if he'd meant to go three times over his data limit this week and telling him his next bill would be over fifty quid. So that made *two* grumpy people.

Personally I thought the zoo was brilliant. We saw lions, monkeys, red pandas, lemurs and loads more. Charlie wasn't quite as impressed. He dragged his feet all day, moaning about how pathetic it was. He didn't even smile when Mum managed to take a photo of me and Dad standing in front of a sign that said '*Warty Pigs*', without us realising. The whole day Charlie was a massive, glowering cloud hanging over our fun.

As we got in the car to drive back to the chalet, Mum said, 'Well, that was amazing!'

'Incredible,' said Dad, who'd eventually got over his mobile bill.

'Not *real* nature though, is it?' said Charlie. 'It's just a big, cruel animal prison.'

WEIRD RELIEF

Finally the train roars into life and we ease our way out of the station. I still feel awful about Hen but, now we're moving, there's also a kind of weird relief in the back of my mind. Charlie and I are on the move again, wherever it is we're going.

I even feel ready to write some poems again. I quickly jot one down about how happy I was to see Charlie again on the platform at Plymouth. It only takes about a minute because the pen just dances across the page. Afterwards I also write down the chant I had in my head back in the alleyway in Exeter. It seems important to do this, even though I'd rather forget all about my panic attack.

As I finish the poems and put my book away, Charlie is really bouncing again. 'Right, well, that's that. Shall we have a biscuit from that tin now? I'm starving.'

How many times . . . ? I think. I hand him the other half of my ham-and-jam butty from this morning and look out of the window as we leave the town behind, crossing a muddle of tracks past rusted-out old engines and dilapidated carriages until the train eventually runs straight.

'*Ladies and gentlemen, welcome to the delayed 15:12 service to Penzance, calling at . . .*' says the cheerful loud-speaker voice. I sit upright and listen as it trawls through the names of towns until it comes to: '*. . . Hayle, St Erth . . .*'

'That's it!' I say, clicking my fingers. 'St Erth. That's our stop. I remember it now. That's where we've got to change trains for St Bernards.'

'So that means we're on the right train?' says Charlie. 'And we're gonna make it?'

'Yep,' I reply, drumming my hands on the table. 'Ha ha! Good news at last.'

This is a pretty amazing coincidence. Of all the trains we could've randomly got on, we chose the right one. At least things are working out for us, even if . . .

There's a bit of a pause when neither of us says anything.

'You could look happier about it,' says Charlie.

I don't reply.

Charlie leans towards me. 'You're not still thinking about that *girl*, are you?'

'Mnyah . . .' I say, wafting my hand towards him.

'Look,' he says, 'this is our trip, right? Just me and you. Epic holiday replay. We don't want some girl we don't even know muscling in on it, do we?'

'I guess not,' I say reluctantly.

'And anyway, if I hadn't dragged you onto this train then it might've been ages till the next one. We might not have made it in time.'

I'm about to tell him that OK, maybe he's right, when I see the conductor come into our carriage. 'Get down!' I whisper. Charlie ducks under the table then crawls under my seat and wriggles out of sight. Sometimes being so tiny has its advantages.

When the conductor reaches us she asks to see my ticket so I show her. I feel quite in control till Charlie starts tickling behind my knees.

I giggle out loud and the conductor raises an eyebrow. 'You all right?' she asks. She's quite young – maybe late twenties. Little bit overweight. Trousers pulled high up over her stomach.

Biting my lip, I back-heel Charlie and he stops.

The conductor studies my ticket and narrows her eyes. 'Preston to St Bernards, eh? Can I . . . ah . . . ask what your name is?'

This is a totally unexpected question. I feel my heart jump. Why does she want to know?

'I . . . My name?' I stammer. My mouth is seriously dry and my brain is blank.

'*Don't tell her*,' whispers Charlie from under the seat. I muffle his voice by coughing and stamping my foot. The conductor tilts her head to one side suspiciously. Blood is pumping into my ears. I need to come up with something quick.

'Wesley . . .' I say, unsure of where this is going. 'Er, Wesley Lizard.'

Why did I say that?

'Wesley . . . *Lizard*?' says the conductor.

'Yes. It's. Er. Italian,' I say, sounding more and more ridiculous with every word. 'My dad was from Italy. He was big in spaghetti.'

Spaghetti?! This is awful.

There's a horrible pause while the conductor taps my ticket with her pencil. Then, sounding unconvinced, she says, 'O-*kay*. Mind how you go then.' She hands me my ticket, then moves away.

As soon as she's gone, Charlie pokes his head up between my knees. '*Ciao*, Wesley,' he says in this ridiculous Italian accent. 'Make-a me some spaghetti or I break-a your face.'

I look at him for a moment. *Wesley Lizard?* What was I thinking? I can't believe she bought it! Before I know it, my shoulders are shaking and my eyes are scrunched up with laughter and I can barely breathe. Then Charlie's face turns serious and he says, 'Uh-oh,' and disappears under the seat again. I look up and stop laughing immediately.

Hen is standing over me. And her face is like thunder. 'What the hell are you doing?' she snarls, sitting down angrily in the seat next to me and dumping her rucksack on the table.

QUESTIONS AND ESCAPES

I don't say anything to her. I don't know what I *can* say. I was kind of hoping Charlie would help me out, but by the time Hen sits down, he's slithered off under the seats. He'll be miles away in no time; he's like a worm.

I'm on my own again.

'That was a really crummy thing to do,' she snaps. 'Leaving me behind after all I've done for you.'

I want to explain but all I can manage is a whispered, 'It was Charlie. He –'

'Your brother?' she says, looking round. 'And where is he now then?'

I glance round just in time to see the toilet door at the end of the carriage closing. Sure enough, a moment later the WC sign lights up to show that the toilet is engaged. *Thanks a bunch*, I think.

'I had to beg them to let me on,' she continues, her voice all angry and teacherish. 'Told the guard on the platform that you've got a terminal illness and I've got your medication.'

'Sorry,' I croak. I realise that I'm hugging my rucksack so

tightly the biscuit tin is digging into my ribs.

'You're *sorry*? Oh, well, that's OK then,' she scoffs, running her hand through her blue hair, 'Wish I'd never bothered.'

Without saying anything, I take off her coat and push it towards her. I hadn't noticed how warm I was until now. 'Here,' I say.

'Unbelievable. I don't care about the flaming coat. I care about . . .' Her voice trails away and she starts again. 'The one time I meet someone who . . .'

Again her voice gives out. She breathes in and out a few times. Then she slaps the table and says, 'Look. Forget it. You and your brother have your stupid holiday. Sorry for helping.'

With that, she snatches the coat from me, shoulders her bag and stomps off along the train, sitting down a few rows away on the other side of the aisle. My stomach feels like lead.

The train rattles on and on, past fields and straggly towns with the sea beyond. After a while, Charlie comes back and dumps himself into his old seat again.

'No, you can't have a biscuit,' I say wearily.

'What did *she* want?'

I shake my head. 'She's mad cos I ran off.'

Charlie leans in. 'We're miles better off without her. Seriously. Look at her hair – I think she might be an alien.'

'An *alien*?'

'Yeah. I saw a programme about them. She probably wants to eat your brain. Anyway, I told you, this is *our* trip so she can get lost.'

'Shh,' I say, but it's obvious when I look over that Hen can hear every word. She's facing away from us, but I can tell that her angry look is back. She's shaking her head and her knuckles are white on the armrest in front.

'No,' says Charlie loudly. 'She needs to leave us alone.'

At that point, Hen suddenly stands up. As she's turning round, Charlie jinks away and back to the toilet again. I feel my body go tense as she marches towards me. Luckily she's blocked off by the conductor, who's appeared from nowhere and is standing over my shoulder.

'Ah, hello again, *Wesley*.' The conductor smiles, bending forward. Hen stands seething in the aisle next to her, waiting for her chance.

'Hi,' I say, trying to ignore Hen and concentrate on the conductor.

The conductor clears her throat awkwardly. 'I've . . . ah . . . rung the police and . . . ah . . . do you have any ID?'

'ID?' I say. 'What do you . . . ?'

'Police have asked all the staff on this line to look out for a boy travelling from Preston to St Bernards. Boy by the name of Martin . . . ah . . . Tompkins. They thought it sounded like a bit of a coincidence when I told them about you.'

The train sways like it's slowing down, and I feel nauseous.

'They told me to double-check before we reach the next stop.'

I make a strange squeaking sound.

'So,' she continues, 'if you could just confirm your name?'

I look around for Charlie. He's out of the toilet again, loitering in the aisle, and he looks back at me, shaking his head. My throat is beginning to tighten. 'I'm . . .'

'Wesley!' exclaims Hen from behind the conductor. 'There you are!'

I turn to her, eyes wide open.

'My brother's such a little ragamuffin,' she chuckles as she squeezes past the conductor and puts her body between us. 'He's always nipping off like this. Come on, this is our stop.'

The conductor looks confused. 'He's your brother. So you're his . . .'

'Sister, yes. That's how it usually works,' says Hen, like she's dealing with an utter imbecile. 'We're the Lizards. Funny name. Dad was Egyptian.'

'*He* said Italian,' says the conductor, confused.

The train brakes hard into the station. The conductor staggers a few steps and collides with Hen.

'Oops, careful,' says Hen pleasantly. 'Dad was both. Moved out from Egypt to Italy to build pyramids. Never caught on, that's why he ended up in England. Anyway. Lovely to chat but we must go.'

I've no idea where we are.

'Come on, *Wes*,' says Hen, pulling me to my feet. Her hand is digging into mine a little bit too hard as she turns to the conductor with a sweet smile. 'Good luck finding this other kid.'

With that, she practically drags me off the train, with

Charlie trailing behind us. We don't look back. On the next platform there's another, smaller train waiting to leave and, without checking where it's going, she pulls me onto it just before its doors close.

STAGE 6

PAR TO NEWQUAY

21 MILES (IN THE WRONG DIRECTION)

TRAIN

QUESTIONS AND SURFBOARDS

The train is pretty rammed. Every other person here seems to be a fluffy-blond-haired dude in shorts or a girl with denim cut-offs and a messy ponytail. We don't even bother to look for somewhere to sit because the only spare seats have bags or surfboards propped up on them. So we stand in between the two clattering carriages, along with more bulky luggage.

'Where are we going?' I ask Hen. I'm wearing the rucksack and I can feel the sharp, comforting corners of the biscuit tin on my back.

'Away from the people who want to find *you*. Now don't move. I'm going in here,' she commands, and she shoves her rucksack down at my feet and disappears into the toilet.

'*This is the 16:15 service to Newquay,*' says a bored, nasal voice over the loudspeaker. A bunch of surf dudes down the carriage cheer at the mention of Newquay. '*Calling at . . .*'

'Aw! I hate Newquay!' whines Charlie. 'I thought we were going to St Bernards. What about the dolphin?'

I do my best to ignore him as he stamps his foot and moans on and on about the zoo and the dolphin.

Newquay. Right. Well, that explains the surfers – everyone knows Newquay's where people go to surf. And I know from our zoo trip that it's not too far from St Bernards, so at least we're going in something like the right direction.

'Look,' I say as patiently as possible, 'we'll be able to change trains and get back to St Bernards in time for high tide. I'm sure of it. Could be much worse. We could've been caught by that conductor, eh?'

Charlie shakes his head. 'If we miss the dolphin cos of that stupid girl . . .'

I smile nervously, my stomach in knots.

For a moment I'm surprised that *I'm* feeling nervous, because I realise I'm not just nervous for him but for me as well. But then I hit upon something that I've probably known deep down all along: that this trip isn't only about him. It's about me too. We both need to see the dolphin again. It feels like I've stepped into a room I'd kept locked from myself. Of course I'm doing it for me, as well as for Charlie. We've got to get there. This is our journey. Our dolphin.

I've tried not to think about the last time I saw it, but the memory suddenly bubbles up in my mind and for the first time I don't push it back down. It's a weird kind of flashback when I replay it – not like any of my other memories. It's not clear like a film, or misty like a dream. It's jagged. Cracked. Like I'm watching it through a shattered window.

NETS AND SWIMMING

The last morning of the holiday. Sunny. Hot, even at seven o'clock. Charlie had got us all out of bed by six. Fiesta stuffed full again, packing more rushed this time, so there are bags on our knees in the back. Chalet keys through the letter box at reception, then driving into St Bernards in silence. Nice and early so no problems getting a parking space. The bay perfect. Tide in. Water emerald clear, waves gently slapping the sea wall. Boats nodding up and down. Mum saying she'd miss this. Handful of tourists walking along the front. Charlie running straight up to the fence, clambering up it and staring out nervously. Biting his lip. Old-Timer strolling along. Saying hello, but Charlie too nervous to reply. Me realising suddenly what this dolphin means to Charlie and why he hated the zoo so much. The dolphin is freedom. Life. The ability to *do*. To live, in the way that Charlie never can. *Don't get too excited. Don't go running off. Make sure you've got your inhaler. You're ill again so you'll have to miss out on that. Why can't you concentrate? Sit there at the table with the thickos.*

And right then I want to hug him. Tell him I love him.

But I don't. Because at that moment the dolphin swims into the harbour. It's Dad who sees it. A black fin. A patch of shade moving slowly among the boats. Charlie yelling. Relief. Happiness. The dolphin rounds the boats and moves into the space ahead of us. Then we see. The tired, laboured swimming. The hoarse, painful cloud of vapour coming out of the blowhole. The tangled orange fishing net trailing from its tail. The vivid scarlet stripe of flesh above its fluke where the net has slashed the skin.

Does it look right at us, or do I imagine that?

All of us concentrating on it too much to notice Charlie slip between the railings. The scuffle of his feet on the ground makes us turn. Desperate shout from Mum catches uselessly in her throat as he plunges, limbs windmilling, ten feet through the air. Awful splash when he hits the water. Flailing arms fighting towards the dolphin. *He can't swim! He can't swim!* Slow progress. Wave lapping over him. Spluttering. Then another wave. Charlie under the water. Dad leaping in after him. Charlie's outline fading as he sinks. Dad ducking down. Grabbing for him. Up for air. Back again. Old-Timer heading after them. Diving gracefully. Perfect entry. Surfacing. Deep breath. Him and Dad going under one more time. This time Charlie pulled up by his ankle. Dad and Old-Timer clutching at a lifebelt someone's thrown. Both men kicking violently with Charlie dragged floppy-doll behind them to the harbour steps. Dad's face hideous with panic. Mum screaming. Howling. Not a human sound. Someone meeting Dad on the steps to help him up. Charlie's body hauled onto the pavement. Face grey. Eyes glassy. Looking at me but not seeing. My hollowed-out insides. Dad pumping on his heart. Old-Timer blowing into his mouth. Mum shaking his arm. Again. Again. Again.

Nothing.

Mum's stopped howling now.

Awful silence.

More blowing. More pumping.

Then a splutter.

Water bursting out of Charlie's mouth like a fountain.

Retching.

Body convulsing.

Onto his side.

Violently sick.

Painful, rasping breaths.

Gulping down air.

Mum clutching him.

Charlie.

ESCAPE AND DEMANDS

The longer we stand between the carriages, the more agitated Charlie gets. He's bouncing up and down nervously and his eyes keep flicking towards the locked toilet door. 'We've gotta get away from her,' he says, nibbling his thumb. 'Why can't you see it? She'll rumble us.'

'Where can we go?' I say. There's no point telling him again that she's helped us out.

His face twitches and he blinks hard behind his specs. 'This was meant to be *our* trip, you know. Me and you. I told you she'd make us late. Now she's dragging us off somewhere stupid. What if –'

'Stop it!' I say. A couple of surf dudes sitting on the floor look up at me. One tells me to *chill*, so I turn my back on them and lower my voice. 'Look, Charlie, I promise we'll see the dolphin tonight, whatever happens. OK?'

I know this is a stupid thing to promise. The ocean isn't an aquarium, like the old man said, right? But I'm desperate. I can't have Charlie running off again.

He knows it's a stupid promise too. 'I'm going over

there,' he sighs, and he picks his way down the aisle, fist-bumping the surf dudes on his way past and saying stuff like, 'Hey, bro, way to ride the gnarly tubes,' and, 'Let's get in motion with the ocean,' in this ridiculous, gravelly American accent. Even when he's in a bad mood he can't resist being a nutter.

I watch as he sits himself down uninvited on the only free seat in the carriage. It's about halfway down, with his back to me, next to a couple of men with dreadlocks and silly trousers who look like they're asleep. Just as he sits down, the toilet door opens and Hen steps out.

'Well done for not running off,' she says sarcastically.

I don't reply. She stares at me for a few moments. 'So, are you going to tell me what all this is about?'

I shrug. 'What do you mean?'

She scratches her head and puts on a dumb voice. 'Er . . . dunno. Maybe, like, *why* are you running away? *Why* are you going to St Bernards? And *why* are the police and a whole bunch of people who work on trains trying to catch you?'

I'm looking at my shoes, moving bits of imaginary dirt around on the floor. 'I'm taking my brother to see a dolphin.'

Hen doesn't say anything, and when I look up at her she's staring at me really hard. Finally she takes a deep breath. When she speaks this time her voice is softer. 'I'm *trying* to help you, Martin. I saw you back there in Exeter and you were –' She sighs, looking for the right words – 'you *scared* me. I couldn't just leave you there like that.'

My face screws up. I don't want to think about what happened in the alleyway.

'Look,' she says, 'just tell me the truth. You can trust me. I read your poem, remember. We're similar, you and me. Our brains work the same way. That's why I had to help. It's your parents, isn't it? You never answered me, back in the alleyway. But it's always parents. That's why *my* head's all over the place. I've been through it all, remember. I've not seen my dad since I was a kid, and as for my mum? Well, let's just say she doesn't approve of anything I do *ever*.'

'I don't know what you're talking about,' I whisper, but it's like someone else is speaking. 'We're just replaying our holiday, that's all.'

'Hang on,' she says. 'Where's your brother?'

Looking towards the floor, I point shakily down the carriage to where he's sitting. Immediately there's a hand under my chin and she's holding my face so I have to look at her.

'Down there. I told you,' I protest, tears prickling behind my eyes, basketball-sized lump in my throat.

She lets go and we stare at each other for what seems like ages. And then her face changes like she's just realised something.

There's a warm pain where her hand was and I'm trying to focus on it because the rest of my body feels like a balloon that's floating through a room of sharp nails, ready to burst at any moment, and I can't breathe without my chest shaking and creaking and she's still staring and maybe Charlie will lend me his inhaler if I ask him and then Hen is speaking and it takes me a few moments to realise what she's saying and when the words finally register with me they just squeeze the breath out of my body and I suddenly know what it feels like to ride a wave like these surfers then have the whole weight of the ocean just crash down on you and my legs give way and my back slides slide down the wall and I'm sitting on the floor.

Time ticks by.

I've covered my eyes with my arms. The rattling of the train is unbearably loud but it isn't loud enough to block out what she says to me next. I can't get away from her words. Even minutes later they echo through me, ricocheting around my skull and slicing through my brain like machine-gun bullets.

'I didn't even think about it at the time, cos I was so mad at you and we were in such a rush,' she said, 'but nobody got on this train with us. And nobody was on the last train with you either. You're on your own.'

STAGE 7

A BENCH ON NEWQUAY TRAIN STATION

TO A BENCH ON NEWQUAY TRAIN STATION

O MILES

SITTING DOWN

THE END OF THE LINE

We've been at Newquay for a while. I'm on a cold metal bench right at the end of the platform, as far away as I can be from the main part of the station. The surf dudes all poured out of here ages ago, shouldering their bags and surfboards and disappearing into the town. There's a faint salty, seaside tang in the air.

The station clock clicks through seven minutes past five. A few people mill about here and there, waiting for trains, but the station seems desolate. Guards are laughing together down the other end of the platform. An old geezer shuffles up and down to kill time. My eyes follow a single plastic bag as it dances past in the wind. It somersaults along the track then gets tangled on the buffers. This is the end of the line.

Hen returns. Sits down next to me. A hot drink in a paper cup is pushed into my hands. 'Here. Drink this. Tea with three sugars.'

I sip it. Too hot.

Hen puts her arm round me. Her body is warm but not soft. 'You're freezing,' she says. I clutch the tea towards my chest and hunch my shoulders. I should really get my jumper out of the rucksack. The clock clicks on through the seconds and minutes. A stationary train on the other platform coughs into life. Lights flicker on inside it. The old geezer walks round to it and climbs on. The plastic bag is stuck on the buffer, flapping uselessly in the breeze.

'Look,' she says. Deep breath. 'I'm sorry. For . . .'

Her voice drifts off. I sip the tea again. Still too hot.

'It's fine,' I say, my voice dry like sandpaper. And then, without looking at her, I start to speak.

I tell her about Charlie. About the holiday. About how he dived in to save the dolphin's life.

'Oh God,' she says, hand over her mouth.

I nod. Then I continue the story.

GOING HOME

Someone had called an ambulance. They wrapped Charlie up in blankets and this tin-foil stuff, then shot off to the nearest hospital, with Mum in the back and me and Dad following in the Fiesta. The drive to Truro seemed to take forever, even though it was only about half an hour.

At the hospital Mum went through with Charlie while I sat in a waiting room watching Dad pace up and down. He was wearing someone else's clothes – a woman had come out of her house and given him her husband's sweater and jeans. They were about three sizes too small. At any other time we'd have made a joke about it.

Finally, sometime in the afternoon, we were allowed to go through and see Charlie. He was propped up in bed looking pale and weak, and holding a grey cardboard bowl in his hands. There were these electric pads wired up to his chest, and machines beeping behind him. It reminded me of that photo of him from when he was born. 'How's it going, bum-face?' I said, trying not to cry.

'Great news.' He grinned. 'I've been picked for the Olympic

swimming team. One of the coaches spotted me. I'm doing the fifty-metres vertical sink.'

We all had a little chuckle at that, because it kind of broke the tension a bit, but then Charlie's laugh sort of morphed into this coughing fit. Really horrible wet coughs they were. Spluttering. Bubbling. The machines started beeping wildly. Mum jabbed at the panic button and in two seconds a nurse and doctor flew through the doors and pulled him upright in bed and smacked his back, and then he spewed up all this water into his cardboard bowl. Slowly he caught his breath and everything settled down again.

'Sorry about that,' said Charlie, wiping the spit away from his mouth. 'Where are my manners?'

I gave a weak smile as the nurse took away the bowl and dropped it into a bin.

'To be on the safe side, we'll keep him in for a while to keep an eye on him,' said the doctor, listening to Charlie's breathing through her stethoscope. 'Especially with his medical history.'

'I'm all right,' said Charlie, but the doctor ignored him.

'Oh, and while I remember,' said the nurse, handing him a fresh bowl, 'someone calling himself *the old-timer* rang. Apparently the dolphin is fine. Some fishermen managed to cut the net off it.'

Charlie gave an enormous grin.

'You're a proper hero,' I said. And I believed it too.

COLD TEA

'Oh, Martin,' says Hen. One hand is still over her mouth. The other has kind of snaked its way around my shoulders. 'You must've been so relieved.'

I swirl my tea round the paper cup then take a gulp. It's cold and disgustingly sweet. I must've been talking for ages.

I know she's looking at me, waiting for me to carry on. Slowly I turn my eyes to meet hers. And there's a split-second when I can tell she's reading something from my face. But I don't want her to read it so I turn away again and suddenly fling the cup as far as I can. It flips over and over, tea flying out of it like brown sparks from a firework. The cup bounces across the tracks and my shoulders crumple. My head flops into my hands. Her fingers dig into my shoulders.

'What's wrong?' she says, but her voice is distant.

My breath seems to come in ragged bursts that tear at my chest and arms. And the words are welling up inside me, forcing their way to the surface like dolphins kicking themselves free, until finally they burst out of my mouth and I start to speak again.

THE CURTAINS

It was almost a week later when it happened. He'd been fine leaving hospital. On fire in fact. He'd only been there two nights but the nurses all came out to see him off. They thought he was brilliant. *Brightened up our lives*, they said. *Wish they were all like him. Breath of fresh air.*

We'd driven the seven hours all the way home and got back to the house in the evening. Then, in the middle of the night, Charlie had pains in his chest. Rushed straight to the A & E at Royal Preston. Checked him over. Night in for observation. But by the morning everything was back to normal. *You've had a big shock. Take it easy. Rest. Come straight back if you notice anything out of the ordinary. Always best to take precautions.*

He was quiet for the rest of the week, sitting on the sofa wearing his PJs and watching back-to-back *Peppa Pig*s on TV, eating his ham-and-jam sandwiches and drawing pictures of dolphins in his little pad. He even joked about how some sick kids get to swim with dolphins and maybe he'd be allowed to do it now.

And then it happened. Nothing dramatic. No fanfares. It just happened.

Thursday morning. I opened the curtains in our room like I always do to wake him up.

And that was it.

He was gone.

I knew it straight away. Cold. Grey. Still. But peaceful. Eyes closed. And on the floor by the side of his bed was his pad. He must've been drawing before he went to sleep. On the open page there was a picture of a leaping dolphin. '*To Martin*,' it said underneath, '*From Charlie.*'

SHADOWS

The plastic bag on the buffers has given up trying to escape. It's dangling limp and still. The train on the other platform eases out of the station.

'Oh, Martin,' Hen says.

I shrug, picking at my thumbnails. I'm surprised that I want to talk about what happened. It's the first time I have, properly. Not that anybody else wants to. Mum and Dad never talk about it. People at school skirt around it like a massive unexploded mine.

Eventually I carry on. 'You know what? No one was even sure exactly what caused it. I mean, his heart *was* rubbish. Always had been. The doctors think it was probably something to do with the shock of going in the water. But maybe it was always going to happen. Maybe it was a bit of both.'

'*Oh, Martin,*' Hen whispers again.

'He's with me all the time, you know,' I say. Hen squeezes me tighter and I realise there are tears running down her cheeks that mix with mine as our faces touch. 'Real as if he was sitting here. I talk to him and he talks back.'

'Like an imaginary friend?' she says. Immediately I think she feels embarrassed to have said this – like it's insensitive or something. But I know what she means.

'No,' I reply. 'More than that. He's a part of me. He's in everything I do. Everything I say. Everything I *think*.'

There's a pause. 'Is that who you were arguing with on the train before? I thought you'd gone . . .' Her voice trails off. She doesn't want to say *mad*.

I understand. 'I'm sorry about running off,' I say. 'He made me do it. I mean, *I* made me do it. I was scared and . . . the part of me that's Charlie didn't want you to find out about all this. It's hard to explain.'

Hen squeezes me tighter. 'You don't have to.'

'Sometimes I can almost touch him,' I say after a long time. 'I even fell onto my backside at Preston station cos I was picturing him tripping over me. He's always there.'

'That's so *sweet*, you know?'

I shake my head. 'Not now it isn't. I need to let him go.'

'Don't say that.'

'Not forget about him. But I need to just, you know, let him rest. We all do. It's been fourteen months. We've got to live, see.' I can feel my voice getting stronger and louder. 'That's all Charlie wanted. To be alive. Like the dolphin. Mum – she can't even get out of bed. Dad – he's never at home; he just works all the time. Me – I keep having these panic attacks like the one you saw. None of us ever even *talk* about Charlie. I know we've lost him, but I want my family back.'

I can feel that my hands have made fists and I'm pounding my knees as I speak. 'You know what? He was cremated and Mum wouldn't let them bury his ashes. We couldn't even say goodbye to him. That's why I've got to go to St Bernards. I *know* that if I go back . . .'

'. . . You'll be able to say goodbye,' says Hen, wiping her nose on the sleeve of her multicoloured coat. 'So when do you need to be in St Bernards?'

'Seven,' I say. We both look at the clock. Five twenty.

'I'll get you there,' she says, standing up. 'Stay here. I'll ask someone.'

ALMOST THERE . . . BUT NOT QUITE

A spider crawled up
The inside of a glass.
It took him all day.
Slithering, sliding on the slippery glass cliff-face,
Sticky liquid weighing him down,
Clogging the tiny hairs on his legs.
He fought and strained,
Desperate to escape.
Three steps forward,
Two steps back,
Until finally he reached the top.
Exhausted, he rested on the lip of the glass.
Then someone took a drink
And swallowed him.

By Martin Tompkins
Aged 13

STAGE 8

NEWQUAY STATION TO A PUB AND BACK AGAIN

ABOUT A MILE

WALKING THERE, SPRINTING BACK

DISAPPOINTMENTS AND SOLUTIONS

I decide to write a poem. I hadn't realised it till now but I'm on the second-to-last page in the exercise book. I'm about to start, my pen hovering over the page, when Hen comes back. Her face doesn't look good. 'Bit of a problem,' she says.

She's right.

It turns out we *can* get to St Bernards but it'll take almost three hours. I can't understand this – I check on my mileage chart and it's only thirty odd miles away – but Hen says that the trains are rubbish round here and you've always got to change somewhere to get somewhere else.

'So we won't get there till eight? But we'll miss high tide,' says Charlie. His voice is suddenly quieter, more distant, like he's on the other side of a window. I turn to look for him like I always do, but he's not there. Not to look at anyway. For a moment I panic, searching all around me. I can't be without him. But then I begin to understand. Talking about him has shifted something.

'This is hopeless,' says Charlie, muffled. And I imagine – but can't see – how he might flop down on the bench with his hands under his chin. 'I feel like a spider stuck in a glass.'

He's right. I can't see him but he's right. This is desperate.

Hen is talking to me. Charlie's voice is wittering on. I know this might not be the time, but before I can do anything about it, the pen is scratching rapidly across the page. I'm writing another poem, about Charlie's spider. I start to feel better, even though the poem's basically about how hopeless everything is.

Writing's how I've managed to cope with everything since last year. It's the only way I know to get my thoughts out. When I finally came back to school, three weeks after the start of term, I was kind of drifting around like a ghost in the corridors and classrooms. Then one day my English teacher, Mr Hendrix, called me in to see him. He said he'd had an idea: a poetry club with one member – me. At first I thought it was stupid, but he told me that I could turn up at his office whenever I fancied it, whether he was there or not. He'd even squared it with my other teachers. If I needed to just wander out of lessons, I could. As long as I was writing he didn't mind. He even gave me a green school exercise book. I asked if I could decorate it, and he said, 'Sure thing, daddy-o,' which is one of his little phrases. I stuck Charlie's last-ever picture on the front of it, then covered it with plastic to protect it.

Without the poetry, without Mr Hendrix, I don't know how

I would've got through the year.

I know that Hen is watching me write. I can feel her wanting to say something, but she waits until I've finished and the book is back in my rucksack.

'Better?' she says.

I nod. She just seems to understand.

'How much money have you got?'

I count it out. Between us we've got eighteen pounds. With her holding my hand, we stride through the station and out into the town. People are buzzing about everywhere, out for the evening, I guess. I stand close to Hen as she argues the toss with a taxi driver.

'No, no,' he says. 'Fifty quid to St Bernards an' that's the best you'll get on a Sat'day, love.'

I can tell she wants to fight him or have a row but she knows this won't do any good. She looks around, then shouts over to some lads who are passing by. Tight T-shirts. Bulging muscles. Gelled hair.

'Hey! Where's the busiest pub with a beer garden round here?' she says.

'We haven't got time for you to have a drink,' I say, but Hen ignores me.

The lads all make *wahey* sounds and say crude things. Hen rolls her eyes. 'In your dreams, boys. Just tell me.'

They say more rude things then walk off laughing, but an older man out with his wife must've overheard. He gives us directions through town and tells us to have a great night, and he hopes I've got some ID on me cos I don't look a day over fourteen, if he's honest.

I wince.

'Right. Let's go,' says Hen.

'Where?' I say.

Hen smiles. 'Pub of course. We gotta earn you a taxi fare, old boy.'

FLAMES

We find the pub no problem. It's a great big place. Music thumping out. Football on big screens inside. Tons of people even though it's still quite early – muscle men, surfers, really lovely-looking girls with tanned legs wearing short skirts. All laughing and drinking, and pouring out onto the wooden deck that overlooks the road. I feel really out of place and nervous, but Hen squeezes my shoulder and tells me everything's going to be fine.

It takes Hen about three seconds to get ready. Rucksack off her shoulders. Coat off. Clubs, sticks and paraffin out onto the pavement. Floppy hat thrust into my hand.

'You got any food?' she asks before she starts. 'I'm starving.'

I don't want to tell her about the omni-special-leftover-from-Christmas biscuits. They're for St Bernards. I said I'd save them and I will. But I've got the ham-and-jam sandwich I made for Charlie still in my rucksack. I really did make the sandwich for him, but of course he wasn't here to eat it. She eyes it uneasily, but once she's had a bite she tells me it's actually delicious and she shovels the rest down in no time.

Then she begins.

Doctor Lizard was right. She is *incredible*. Without any introduction she just starts. She begins by flinging the clubs in the air, four of them spinning, crossing them over, catching them backhand, forehand, behind the back, arcing throws that loop high into the air, hands placed perfectly to catch. Eyes closed then open again. A growing sense of realisation and appreciation from the pub. People nudging each other and turning round. Others pressing from inside to see. Then she catches three clubs before bending forward and catching the other one on the back of her neck. Massive applause. A bow.

Then out come the sticks and she pours some paraffin onto them before slipping the little bottle into her back pocket. The crowd says *oooh*.

'Who's got a lighter?' she calls out. I know already that she's got one, but this must be part of the act. A big bloke comes out and holds one up for her. His mates cheer. He lights the first stick with a *whumph*.

'Stay here. You're perfect,' she says, lighting the other three sticks off the first one. 'Stand up straight. Hold these. Don't move. I don't want you to die.'

She's speaking to him, but really she's talking to the audience. The big bloke's mates laugh loud and hard but he does what she says, holding the sticks out wide as the flames dance up into the air. Then she climbs up him like a ladder and sits on his shoulders before taking the sticks off him in one hand.

'Hold this leg and this hand,' she says firmly, offering him her free hand. The flaming sticks are held as far away as possible in the other.

Big Bloke looks surprised. Worried. The crowd go tense. And in a few seconds she's crouching on his shoulders. Bit of a wobble. Then she's standing up slowly and letting go of his hand. Big Bloke's trying not to look like he's straining as he grips her ankles. A small cheer. And Hen starts to juggle. Four flaming sticks dancing through the sky. Then she catches all of them and produces the bottle from her back pocket. A quick gulp and a hard blow on the sticks. A ball of flame erupts through the air. There's an enormous cheer before she leaps off Big Bloke's shoulders, lands on the ground and bows.

'Go round with the hat. *Quick*,' she hisses, pushing me towards the terrace as the crowd goes wild. She puts the torches out on her tongue and holds up Big Bloke's arm. He gives her a kiss on her cheek. And meanwhile I'm on the terrace, edging between bodies, tables, chairs. Money rains into the hat *chink-chink-chink*. One of Big Bloke's mates even drops in a tenner, and the hat's getting fuller and heavier till Hen yells, 'Martin. Police. Let's go.'

And the people part to let me through and we're sprinting along the streets, laughing our heads off, the hat clutched to my chest. All I can think about is one thing: Charlie would LOVE this.

STAGE 9

NEWQUAY TO ST BERNARDS

31 MILES

(TAXI)

QUIET AND BISCUITS

The taxi swings through the suburbs of Newquay and soon we're out onto the main road. It's dusk now and the other cars are putting on their lights. The *euphoric* feeling I had because of the juggling and the money didn't last long. Back at the station it was time for business. Huddled on a bench, we counted the money – sixty-two quid including what we already had. *Not bad*, said Hen. She asked if I wanted some grub or anything, but I said not now and, once we'd agreed a fare and shown our money to the driver, we were straight into the first cab in the line.

Now here we are. I feel nervous and a bit subdued. I haven't said anything in the ten minutes since we climbed inside. To keep myself going, I've looked at my mileage chart and added up all the distance I'll have travelled today. It should've been 370 miles, but it'll be more like 421 by the time we get there, if I count all the walking and running and wrong trains as well.

My rucksack is on the seat next to me, with Hen on the other side. She squeezes my hand over the top of it and smiles at me. The clock in the cab blinks onto six twenty.

'How long will it take?' I say.

The taxi driver rubs his neck. 'Hard to say that, boy. 'Nother forty-five minutes, give or take.'

I bite my lip.

Hen's got her phone in her hand, spinning it round in her fingers. A couple of times she taps it and her finger hovers over the glowing screen. Then she pulls it back to her chest and screws up her face.

'Will we be there in time, Marty?' Charlie says. His voice is tiny now. A thin, reedy whisper somewhere near my heart.

'Don't worry,' I say. Hen glances at me, but I think she knows who I'm talking to. 'I know high tide's at seven, but the water'll still be in for a while after that. We'll see it. I promise.'

But can I promise this? Will the dolphin be there? The ocean's not an aquarium, remember.

No. Got to be positive. Got to believe.

I want to write a poem to settle me down, but I can't. There's only one page left in the book and I feel like it needs to be something special. Something to round everything off.

'Can I have one of them biscuits now?' Charlie says, and I laugh to myself, wiping a tear from my eye.

Hen glances at me for a moment, and she looks like she's about to cry too. At first I think she must've heard Charlie as well, but then she taps her phone again and holds it to her ear, biting her thumbnail.

'Hi, Mum,' she says, her voice straining. 'It's me. Henrietta.'

She takes a deep breath and I squeeze her hand. It takes her ages before she can go on. 'I'll come home and see you tonight. No. I want . . . I mean I'll *try* to stay this time. It's . . . I met this kid and . . . Look, I can't explain right now. No. I can get the train. Wesley'll pick me up. Mum . . . I . . .' It sounds like she's going to say something else, but then she stops herself and says, 'I'll tell you later.'

She hangs up and leans her head onto my shoulder. When I glance down I can see that her face is wet with tears.

ARRIVING AND PARKING

I remember the outskirts of St Bernards perfectly. How could I forget them? The caravan sites and supermarkets that slowly melt into the arcades and hotels and beach shops and art galleries and pubs and cafes.

'Where d'you wanna be then?' says the driver. It's the first thing he's said for about half an hour.

'Harbour, please,' I reply, and he sucks his teeth like I've asked him to drop us on the moon. We nip down a few steep, narrow streets, avoiding the late-season tourists who walk along the middle of the road. At one point we take a wrong turn down a one-way. The driver swears, reverses and pulls over outside a shop. 'Harbour's two minutes that way.' He points. 'This is as far as I'll go.'

It takes him a painfully long time to count through the coins we give him. When he's finally done, we grab our bags, then sprint down to the harbour. It's getting much darker now. The sun is low, its rippling reflection turning the water into liquid gold. The memories of the town flood back to me. The smell of fish and chips. The hoards of greedy seagulls.

It's like the last year never happened.

But it did of course.

I slip my rucksack off and hold it to my chest. The biscuit tin is hard against my ribs. Not yet. Not yet.

I press myself against the fence and scan the harbour. Nothing. I stare and bite my lip and I can't see it. *Why isn't it there?*

But then.

'What's *that*?' asks Hen, beside me.

Sure enough.

A knot of people further along are pointing out to sea, making the tell-tale whoops and gasps. I follow their fingers. And there it is! The dolphin! It's back! Skimming through the sparkling water, its fin slicing the gold. But *hold on* . . . there's a small shape alongside it.

'*A baby as well!*' whispers Charlie inside my heart. His voice is crackly. Little more than a breath. 'A baby, Martin! Look at it.'

'I've never . . . It's . . .' says Hen but she can't finish the sentence because the dolphins are swimming towards us and Hen's totally mesmerised.

I can see a dark stripe – a scar – on the mother's tail, just above the fluke. 'It's the same one!' I shout. 'It's Charlie's dolphin!'

And the bag is on the floor. And the omni-special-leftover-from-Christmas biscuit tin is in my hands. And my fingernails are under the lid. And I've lifted it off. And –

'Martin! What are you doing?!' cries a voice behind me.

I spin round and freeze. Mum, Dad and a policeman are striding towards us.

BISCUITS

'What are you *doing*?' she repeats as she clutches me tightly, the tin hard between us.

'I . . . I . . .' I begin, but before I know it we're both shaking and crying.

'I'll leave you to it,' says the policeman. He tips his hat to my mum and dad then strides off. Nobody acknowledges him leaving.

'We've been so worried,' sobs Mum, and the words come tumbling out breathlessly. 'The alarm on your phone was going off but you weren't there, and I found the paper with the journey times. Then I remembered how that teacher rang up last week saying he was scared you'd do something like this.' She takes a breath then carries straight on. 'So I ran to the train station and they said they'd seen you. Then the police put out a call and a policewoman travelling down south said she'd seen you acting funny. So we called the train companies and –'

'We went straight to Manchester Airport,' says Dad, his hand resting on my shoulder. 'We knew where you were going, son, and there was a flight so . . . you know . . .'

And just as I'm thinking that this is the longest conversation I've had with my mum and dad in a whole year, Mum lets go of me. Her eyes flick downwards. There's a beat, like she's realised something she knew all along. Then, very gently, her hands slip over the sides of the omni-special-leftover-from-Christmas biscuit tin and she tries to prise it out of my hands.

'No!' I say, yanking it back from her and pressing the lid back on. I'm surprised by the power of my voice. 'You're not having it!'

Mum stares at me in shock.

'Come on, son,' says Dad, but I struggle out from under his hand.

'*Please*, Martin,' Mum begs, and I look at her – *really look at her* – for the first time in a year. Oh. She's aged. She used to have plump cheeks, but she's lost so much weight they're hollow. And her skin is pale and dull from being indoors all year. And there are rings round her eyes and now she's crying, her weak shoulders shaking with each sob. 'Please. Please.'

'Jeez, Martin, just let her have a biscuit,' says Hen, like I'm the cruellest person in the world. And somewhere, deep inside me, I can just about hear Charlie sadly laughing.

'They're not *biscuits*!' cries Mum, turning to face Hen. 'That's my son!'

THE TRUTH

Hen's eyes look like they're about to pop out of her head.

I say nothing.

'How *could* you?' howls Mum. 'How could you . . .'

Suddenly she's whacking my chest and I'm just standing there, gripping the box and taking it until the blows get lighter and lighter and she breaks down and Dad pulls her off me and holds her to him.

'You should never have done this, Martin,' says Dad over her shoulder.

And that's it.

The final straw.

I've had enough.

'I did it for you!' I shout, 'I did it for the family! I did it for us!'

'Don't you shout at me,' Dad snarls, finger up towards my chest.

Hen steps in front of him. 'Leave him alone.'

Dad looks down and seems to notice her for the first time. 'What's it got to do with you?'

Hen ignores the question. 'What's he done? I don't get it. Why are you screaming at him?'

Dad's body stiffens.

There's a tense silence. I take a deep breath. And then I tell her. Slowly and softly. 'I stole Charlie's ashes. From the jar . . . the *urn* on the mantelpiece. I put them in the biscuit tin. And I ran away.'

'How could you?' sobs Mum again.

'You don't get it do you?' I yell. 'Charlie's dead. *Dead.*'

'Stop it!' cries Mum, burying her head in Dad's chest.

But I won't stop. Not now. 'He wouldn't want to sit there on the mantelpiece in a stupid tub. He'd want to be . . .'

I cast my arm across the harbour. Behind me, the sun is sinking lower. The dolphin is still there, splashing around just metres away from us. The tourists are still pointing at it and cooing like we don't exist.

'No!' says Mum. 'No. He needs to be with us. With his family.'

'But he'll always be with us,' I said. 'We'll never forget him, will we? How could we? He's in all of us, all the time. But we've got to say goodbye.'

'No!' says Mum, and her hands are on the tin again but now her grip is weaker.

'He'd want us to live, Mum,' I say. 'He'd want us to be alive like the dolphin.'

A few moments pass. Then Dad looks at me and his face folds into a frown. 'Hang on,' he says. 'The alarm going off on your phone to wake us up. The train times right next to it. The way you left the lid off your brother's urn so we'd see what you'd done. The tin gone but the tray of biscuits left behind . . .' He pauses. 'You wanted us to follow you, didn't you?'

The question stops me like a hand in the chest. I open my mouth and my lips try to form an answer, but the truth is that I really don't know. Maybe I did. Maybe I wasn't running away from Mum and Dad at all. Maybe I was running towards them.

Dad gently places his hand on my shoulder and Mum tilts her head to one side and looks at me, a bit like how Charlie used to do.

I feel my eyes drawn to the water. And for the first time Mum and Dad seem to notice the dolphin. It's right by the harbour wall, playing with its baby. They're flipping and twisting and corkscrewing over each other.

I've no idea how long we stand there. Time doesn't seem important any more. But, ever so slowly, Mum's fingers slip off the tin and she turns to me. There's a terrible moment when I think she's going to scream again, but then she just leans forward and kisses the tin and whispers goodbye, then she nods her head and puts her hand over her mouth. I realise that everything has changed.

'Do it quick,' she whispers, her eyes screwed up and her shoulders shaking. 'Do it quick, Marty.'

'Go on, son,' says Dad grimly, and he pats me on the arm. 'For Charlie.'

I turn to Hen. She's wiping her eyes. Her make-up has run down her cheeks but she smiles at me through her tears.

And Charlie's there again, right there, in front of me, in my heart and all around me. And his voice is as strong as it ever was. 'Can I swim with the dolphin now, Marty?' he grins. 'Can I?'

I rip the lid off the tin and I stare at the grey powder inside that used to be my brother. Then, without looking at anyone else, I turn and tip it out over the railings. And a gust of wind catches Charlie's ashes and swirls them out over the water in a beautiful silver cloud.

Then something incredible happens. Or perhaps it doesn't happen. Perhaps I imagine it. But it doesn't matter because, for one beautiful moment, what I imagine and what's real are one and the same thing.

With an enormous splash of spray that catches the light, the baby dolphin leaps out of the water and into the sky, right through Charlie's cloud. It hangs in the air for a moment, whipping the ashes into dancing whirls that mingle with the golden drops of water, before it plummets down and disappears into the dark sea. A spray of tiny droplets scatter down onto the water afterwards, churning and rippling on the surface.

And now I know what my final poem will be.

LEAPING DOLPHIN, PART 2

Your life is a leaping dolphin.
A brief moment of
Exquisite beauty and possibility
Before you return to blankness.
Blackness.
But after you land
And disappear,
Those tiny golden droplets of water
That each carry your reflection
Shower down,
Creating endless ripples
That spread out forever,
Colliding endlessly
And mingling together to form
A permanent reminder of who you are.
Charlie.
My brother.

By Martin Tompkins
Aged 13

ABOUT THE AUTHOR

Mark Lowery is the author of several books for children and young adults, including the Roman Garstang Adventures. He has been longlisted for the Branford Boase Award and shortlisted for several prizes, including the Children's Book Award and the Roald Dahl Funny Prize. He grew up in Preston and now lives near Cambridge with his young family.

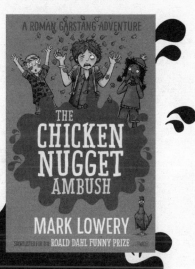

MORE GREAT BOOKS
BY MARK LOWERY

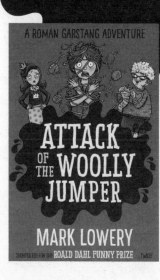

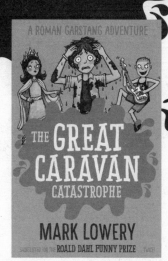

Thank you for choosing a Piccadilly Press book.

If you would like to know more about our
authors, our books or if you'd just like to know
what we're up to, you can find us online.

www.piccadillypress.co.uk

You can also find us on:

We hope to see you soon!